A Little
Christmas
Spirit

A Little

Christmas

Spirit

SUSAN BUCHANAN

Copyright

First published in 2024 by Susan Buchanan
Copyright © 2024 Susan Buchanan
Print Edition

This novel is a work of fiction. Names and characters are the product of the author's imagination and any resemblance to actual persons, living or dead, is entirely coincidental.

A CIP catalogue record of this title is available from the British Library
Paperback – 978-1-915589-02-6

Dedication

For Bill Cobley
The best father-in-law a girl could ask for
And the inspiration for Stanley

About the Author

Susan Buchanan lives in Scotland with her husband, their two young children and a crazy Labrador called Benji. She has been reading since the age of four and had to get an adult library card early as she had read the entire children's section by the age of ten. As a freelance book editor, she has books for breakfast, lunch and dinner and in her personal reading always has several books on the go at any one time.

If she's not reading, editing or writing, she's thinking about it. She loves romantic fiction, psychological thrillers, crime fiction and legal thrillers, but her favourite books feature books themselves.

In her past life she worked in International Sales as she speaks five languages. She has travelled to 51 countries and her travel knowledge tends to pop up in her writing. Collecting books on her travels, even in languages she doesn't speak, became a bit of a hobby.

Susan writes contemporary romantic fiction, partly set in Scotland, usually featuring travel, food or Christmas, but always with large dollops of friendship, family and community. When not working, writing or caring for her two delightful cherubs, Susan loves reading (obviously), the theatre, quiz shows and eating out – not necessarily in that order!

You can connect with Susan via her website www.susan buchananauthor.com or on Facebook www.facebook.com/susancbuchananauthor and on Twitter @susan_buchanan or Instagram authorsusanbuchanan.

Acknowledgements

Huge thanks to

Wendy Janes for editing www.wendyproof.co.uk

Claire at Jaboof Design Studio for my gorgeous cover. Ha – you thought you couldn't beat the previous covers, but you've done it again!

Paul Salvette and his team at BB Ebooks for book formatting www.bbebooksthailand.com

Catherine Ferguson, Katy Ferguson, Heather Harkin, Susan Allan, Anne Pack for agreeing to beta read for me.

The Procrastinators Begone

The Scottish chapter of the Romantic Novelists' Association

The Romantic Novelists' Association – generally!

My ever-expanding Advance Review team

Rachel's Random Resources for always providing such wonderful blog tours and all the amazing bloggers who take part.

Sue Baker of the Riveting Reads and Vintage Vibes Facebook group for my launch day celebration

Thanks to the following Facebook groups:

Lizzie's Book Group, run by the amazing Lizzie Chantree, for constant support.

The Friendly Book Community

Chick Lit and Prosecco, run by Anita Faulkner

To all of my super-supportive fellow authors who kindly help spread the word – I have your back, and I know you have mine!

Most important of all – the fam. To my son and daughter for putting up with me having my office door closed to write sometimes, and bearing with me when I'm on a deadline, and to my husband, for leaving me to get on with it!

And last, and by absolutely no means least, my readers. Thank you for continuing to invest in my books. It means the world to me, as do your lovely comments. If you want to connect with me about my books, you can always email me on susan@susanbuchananauthor.com

Chapter One

'Mum, come on.' Lara put her woollen-mittened hand in her mum's as they approached the school's main entrance.

'Welcome to Heatherwood. I'm Mrs Ralston. The assembly hall is this way.'

Lara led her mum down to the assembly hall where the Christmas fair was being held. She had loved helping the teachers decorate it this week. It was like a winter wonderland. Strings of snowflakes dangled from the ceiling, and her year group had frosted pine cones and twigs and placed them around the edges of the hall to make it look like a forest floor in winter. They'd even covered the stage in fake snow yesterday – they'd had to wait to do that, though, as some classes had PE on a Friday afternoon, and their assembly hall was also their games hall.

'Oh, Lara, did you do all this?' her mum asked as they entered the hall.

She glanced up at her mum, whose eyes were shining. 'I helped. I put the baubles on all the branches of that tree over there.' She pointed to one of the five smaller Christmas trees in the room. 'And I made some paper chains.' She gestured to a display area on the right.

'You've all done such a fantastic job,' her mum said.

'Thanks. I wish I was an elf helper though. Some of the

primary sevens get to be elves.'

'Don't worry, Lara. I'm sure you'll get to be an elf when you're in P7.'

Lara hoped so. It just felt a very long way off. And she was nine. Surely she could help just as well as someone who was ten. At least her mum was letting her help with taking the money for any jewellery she sold.

Her mum had insisted on viewing the stall before bringing in her jewellery from the car. She wanted to see how much space she had to display everything. She'd also agreed Lara could help dress the stall to make it look nice.

'There are quite a few stalls,' her mum said. 'Do you know which one is ours?'

Lara nodded and tugged her mum's hand, dragging her to the other side of the room, next to the face-painting area.

When they arrived at their stand, her mum sighed.

'Are you OK, Mum?'

'Yes, darling, everything's fine. It's just that we're going to have quite the queue in front of our stand, and I'll bet it's not to buy jewellery. There's always huge queues for face painting at these things.'

'Can I have my face painted?' Lara asked. She really wanted to have her face done up as an elf, even if she couldn't be an elf helper this year.

'Of course. Now, let's figure out what we're going to bring in from the car and we can set up the stand. It's only an hour until the fair opens. And once we're done we can grab a hot chocolate from the van outside.'

Lara smiled. That sounded perfect. 'What time is Uncle Jacob coming?'

'He said he'd be here soon. He texted to say he and Aunt Sophie have to pick up the cakes from Sugar and

Spice to bring for their stall.'

When her mum looked around as if she'd lost something, Lara said, 'What is it?'

'I was wondering where the Sugar and Spice stall is.'

'Oh, I know. It's the one near the door.'

'Ah, well, they're bound to sell lots of their cakes then.'

'Do I get one too?' Lara asked.

Her mum rested her hand on her shoulder. 'Of course. When have I ever come between you and Uncle Jacob's cakes?'

'It is kinda cool having an uncle who owns a bakery,' said Lara.

'Indeed. Who'd have thought he'd be here, with a stall, let alone running the best bakery café in town. If he hadn't had the courage to ask Natalie for a job all those years ago, when I was pregnant with you, we wouldn't be living in Winstanton now.'

'That would be terrible,' Lara said. 'Oh, look, there he is now.' She pointed to the door of the games hall where her uncle Jacob and aunt Sophie were striding towards them with beaming smiles and trays of cakes covered in clingfilm.

'Uncle Jacob.' Lara ran towards him and he hugged her to him, precariously balancing his tray of cakes between one hand and his body before she released him and barrelled into her aunt Sophie, who had chosen that moment to put her tray on a table.

'Hi, Tabs,' said her uncle. 'I see you've not set up yet either.'

Lara's mum hugged her brother and said, 'No, we've just arrived. I wanted to get the lay of the land before I brought everything in.'

'Good plan, Tabitha,' said Sophie. 'Why don't we walk back together to the car park and pick everything up?'

'Am I allowed one of those vanilla cupcakes?' asked Lara in a pleading tone.

Her uncle Jacob smiled at her. 'If you help me carry the next lot in, I'll set a cupcake aside for you.'

As they walked back through the hall, Sophie said, 'Isn't it gorgeous in here? So festive. Jacob, we'll have to watch out or Sugar and Spice will have some serious competition.'

'Oh, I'm all for a little friendly competition, especially at Christmas. And this is all for a good cause. Plus, let's face it, once they've tasted my divine creations–' he paused for effect '–no one will be able to resist coming to the café to try out the new Christmas range.'

'Uncle Jacob, don't be silly. Everyone comes to Sugar and Spice anyway. Everyone knows you bake the best cakes.'

'Lara, you are my best advertisement. Who needs marketing when you have a niece?'

'Yes, quite, but not too many sweets for this one, please, Jacob. We've already had the Tooth Fairy visit once this week,' Lara's mum said.

Jacob raised his eyebrows. 'Tooth Fairy? Really? Go on then, let's see.'

Lara opened her mouth to show the gap in her front teeth.

'Oh, wow,' Sophie said, 'you'll be able to sing that song "All I Want For Christmas is My Two Front Teeth".'

Lara looked at her, her brow knitted in confusion.

'I think that one went right over her head,' her uncle Jacob said, patting her aunt on the arm.

Back in the car park, her mum opened the boot, took out two small boxes and handed them to her, then picked up a huge box, which she balanced on her hip as she closed the boot. 'Come on, let's get this stall set up.'

'Did I hear there was a mulled wine stand?' asked her aunt Sophie. 'I love mulled wine.'

'Yes, but that's for afters, and let's hope they have a non-alcoholic version,' Uncle Jacob said.

'What's mulled wine?' Lara asked as they carried the boxes indoors.

'Ah, that's for adults,' her mum said. 'Anyway, Jacob, I think Lara might have done enough to deserve that cupcake. Do you agree?'

'Absolutely. Lara, once you've helped your mum set up, come over to our stand and you can have one.'

'Thanks, Uncle Jacob. Mum, where should I put this?' She was keen to finish so she could take her uncle up on his cupcake offer. Vanilla was her absolute favourite, especially the frosting.

Fraser wandered around the hall, taking in the variety of stalls and the chatter and atmosphere around him. Half an hour in, and so far, it looked like a successful fair. His staff had put a callout to parents asking for artisans and small businesses to come peddle their wares, and they'd also done a great job of creating the perfect Christmas-themed backdrop. He particularly liked the frosty background in pale blue with embossed white snowflakes. That and the twinkling stars really helped create the right ambiance in amongst all the festive stalls.

Mrs Dalwood was currently manning the children's

personally created Christmas mementoes: photo frames, magnets, Christmas cards, bookmarks, tree decorations. Any money raised would go to the children's summer fair, where the school tended to go large and hire a bouncy castle and other equally fun pieces of play equipment.

The children had been working hard during the second part of November to ensure they had as many different types of crafts and by as many children as possible. Everyone had contributed something.

As Fraser turned, he noted scores more people pouring in and a wave of satisfaction swept through him.

Since everything was going well, he decided it was time for him to taste the delights of the bakery stand, Sugar and Spice. He knew they had a shop in town. He'd walked past it a few times.

'Hi, there. This all looks marvellous,' Fraser said.

'Thanks.'

'This is the headmaster, Mr McCafferty,' whispered a little girl to his side. He'd seen her around the school, although he didn't know her name. It took a long time to learn well over two hundred names and he'd only been headmaster at Heatherwood for a couple of months. Those who behaved tended to fly below his radar.

'Is that so?' Jacob held out his hand. 'Jacob Field.'

'Pleasure to meet you, Jacob. Your stand smells amazing, and you have such an incredible range of cakes, I don't know what to choose.' He paused then asked the girl, 'What can you recommend?'

'I like the vanilla cupcakes best, but apparently adults like different cakes to children.'

'Really?' Fraser said.

'Yes! Like teera may su.'

Fraser smiled. 'I quite like tiramisu, but I also like cupcakes.'

The girl's eyes widened in surprise, then she said, 'Oh, I'd better go. I need to go and help Mum. You should come see our stall, too, Mr McCafferty. It's next to the face painting.'

Fraser smiled. 'I will.'

As she raced off, Fraser suddenly realised Jacob had been describing some cakes to him, and mortified that he'd been daydreaming, he hastily pointed to a selection and Jacob boxed them up.

'I'll have one myself and then I'll take a couple to my mum. It was nice to meet you, Jacob.'

'You too, Mr McCafferty.'

After walking up and down the six aisles of stalls, Fraser finally arrived at Lara's mum's stall, but Lara wasn't there; instead he saw a woman, who had her back to him, moving around some boxes.

He looked at the items laid out on her stall, then glanced at the name – Tabitha's Trinkets. Tabitha. An unusual and relatively old-fashioned name. He liked it. He cleared his throat, and Tabitha, he assumed, turned and said, 'I'm sorry, I didn't realise anyone was there.'

'No problem. How's trade going today?'

'Pretty well, thanks. I wasn't sure how it would go as I usually sell a range of slightly different goods at upmarket craft fairs. Fortunately, there does seem to be a demand here for Christmas-themed glass jewellery.'

'Your pieces are very nice,' Fraser said, wishing he could take back the term 'very nice'. It was so unoriginal.

Tabitha looked at him as if she could see into his very soul, and he felt heat rise in his face.

'Actually, could I take this brooch?'

'The nutcracker?' Tabitha said.

'Yes, it's a gift for my mum.'

Tabitha boxed it for him, saying, 'I hope your mum likes it. Enjoy the rest of the fair.'

'Oh, I will,' said Fraser.

As he walked away, he knew the Christmas fair couldn't get any better.

Chapter Two

'Paul, I can't stay long. It is Saturday, after all, and I know I like to have a nosey to see the new stalls and pick up a few Christmas gifts, but I told Christine and Susan I'd go shopping with them in Glasgow this afternoon.'

Paul turned to his wife, tamping down his impatience. She'd only arrived two minutes earlier and she was already complaining and desperate to get away. Why couldn't she just appreciate the start of the Christmas preparations?

'Elaine, I'll have to stay to lock up. Besides, I love the Christmas fair. Maybe you can get a lift to the station if you see someone you know.' Whenever they were out together, it certainly felt like she knew everyone in Winstanton.

'You couldn't drop me off?' Her voice was wheedling now and it was beginning to affect his mood. He and the kids had spent ages decorating the foyer, the corridors and the games hall – the latter specifically for the fair – but all Elaine was interested in was waltzing off to Glasgow for yet more shopping with her two sisters who were visiting from England.

Firm for once, he said, 'Sorry, love, I can't. I have to be on-site for the whole fair. If you can't get a lift, you could call a taxi.'

Elaine's face fell, but Paul had decided he was going to

enjoy this fair, despite his wife's lack of enthusiasm for it.

'Fine,' Elaine said. 'Which stalls are here this year anyway?'

Paul smiled. He knew how to reel his wife in. 'Oh, you'll have to go and see for yourself. Shall we? It's getting busier. Bear in mind it has been open for well over an hour. You'll need to get a move on or all the good stuff will be gone.'

That galvanised Elaine into action – she was nothing if not a savvy shopper, and she hated to miss out on a bargain, or the latest thing.

She wandered off down the corridor towards the games hall as Paul took a long look around the foyer, where he and the kids had added two five-foot nutcrackers to the welcome area the day before. Primary six and seven had been working on them for the past few weeks and had been beaming with pride when the headteacher had unveiled them at assembly.

Paul wasn't sure what he thought of the new head yet. He was rather formal, which wasn't really in keeping with the tone the rest of the staff at Heatherwood took towards each other, and he was young, too, which seemed at odds with his whole demeanour. Yet, the day before, he'd smiled at the unveiling, and the kids had been in raptures at his comments about their handiwork.

As he walked down the corridor, he passed primary four's snowmen paintings, primary three's Christmas trees and the baubles drawn and painted by those in primaries one and two – which adorned the walls on the approach to the games hall.

Perhaps his wife wasn't feeling Christmassy, but when he witnessed the effort the kids put into their work for the festive season, he certainly did.

It was even more in evidence in the games hall, which had truly come alive with the bustling stalls – he loved how everyone in the community came together and not only sold their wares, but really got into the Christmas spirit, whether they'd decorated their stalls with Christmas paraphernalia, or donned a whole Christmas-themed outfit, or gone for a more subtle approach with festive earrings. It always made his heart sing to see everyone embrace the season and the school's opening Christmas event.

With a pang, he wondered how many more of these events he'd attend as janitor of the school. Not many, if Elaine had anything to do with it.

She hadn't even realised he hadn't followed her in. He spotted her now, weaving in and out of the stalls, already taking out her purse to buy something.

He took the opportunity to cast his eyes around the hall, drinking in the atmosphere. Smiles were in full force as neighbours and friends chatted and oohed and aahed over the selection of potential Christmas gifts on offer. He decided to wander round and let Elaine do her own thing – she would anyway.

Maybe he'd manage to pick up a few stocking fillers himself.

Ah, there was his favourite stall. Sugar and Spice. They also owned his favourite café in the town.

'Hello, Jacob, how are you?' Paul said, stopping beside the Sugar and Spice stall and taking in the unusual array of treats. That's what he liked about their bakery – it always had something new to offer you, didn't stick with the same old tried and tested flavours.

'Paul, you're looking well,' Jacob said as he pushed his

floppy hair out of his eyes. Paul had a soft spot for Jacob. Sometimes he'd drop in to his office when he came to pick Lara up if Tabitha was working away, and bring a selection of goodies for him and the staff to try. He called him and the staff his tasters. Personally, Paul thought if he kept plying him with delicious cakes, he was happy to be his guinea pig forever. Sugar and Spice never failed to produce something that made his tastebuds sing, and he loved the stories behind the cakes too. And that had all started with Natalie, who was the one who'd talked the previous owner, Mrs Williams, into hiring Jacob in the first place.

'Thanks, Jacob. And I'm sure I'll feel even better when I've tucked into one of these later.' He pointed towards a row of cakes resembling tiny tiramisu. 'What are those?'

'Ah, that one is for after dinner, it's a *Pio Quinto*, from Nicaragua.'

'Nicaragua! And how did you come across that recipe?'

'Actually, it was a guy I went to school with; his dad was a diplomat over here. I heard from him last year for the first time in almost a decade, and it inspired me to look up their Christmas cakes. We've already made a lot of the European ones, so I thought why not try further afield.'

'Good plan. And what about that one?'

'*Drømmekage* from Denmark. Soft sponge with coconut topping.'

'Hmm,' Paul said. 'I'm not a huge coconut fan.'

'Well, I think this one would convert you. Here, I have a few samples. Try one.' Jacob handed Paul a piece to try and he popped it in his mouth.

'Is that caramelised?' Paul said once he'd let the cake slip down.

'Yep,' said Jacob. 'Tabs and Lara love it. Lara calls it

bedtime cake as it means "sweet dream".'

'Is that so? Well, you learn something new every day. I'm not surprised they love it though – it's delicious. OK, you have yourself a convert. Can I take a piece of that as well as the Nicaraguan one, and what's that one? It looks incredible.'

Paul knew he really shouldn't allow himself any more – maybe he'd share with Elaine – but the strawberry-topped whipped cream concoction with mistletoe on top had drawn his attention. It almost looked too pretty to eat, but he'd give it a go.

'That is *kurisumasu keki* from Japan. Eye-catching, isn't it?'

'It sure is. If it's not too much trouble, could I have a slice of that, too, please, and then I'd better behave myself, or I'll have to go on a treadmill for a month.'

Jacob laughed. 'We can't have that. Is that what you intend doing when you retire, taking up going to the gym?'

'No! Do I look like a gym bunny?'

When Jacob didn't reply, Paul hid a smile. He knew not to take offence. Jacob didn't have a bad bone in his body – they could do with more like him around. Jacob was eternally cheerful and pleasant to everyone around him. No wonder Mrs Williams had jumped at the chance when she was selling up to have Jacob and Tabitha buy her out. She knew they'd look after her business, as since the moment Jacob arrived, he'd been a hit with the customers.

'Ha, you and me both, Paul. No, I prefer a run. Can't be doing with being stuck indoors. I'm already indoors most days, baking, but I need to run off these cakes, too, you know.' Jacob patted his washboard-flat stomach. Paul remembered when his had been like that – a long time ago.

'I'm with you. Anyway, retirement's a long way off, thankfully, so I don't need to make any gym-frequenting decisions quite yet.'

Jacob's eyebrows scrunched up. 'Oh? I thought you were retiring after the summer.'

'No chance. There's life left in the old dog yet. Whatever gave you that idea?'

Jacob coloured and eyed the floor. 'Just something I overheard. I must have got it wrong.'

Now Paul was worried. Were the school making him retire? He knew he would be of age, but he'd had a chat with the previous head before she went on maternity leave, and had told her he'd like to stay on for a few years past retirement. He loved the school, loved the kids, loved the environment. Being put out to pasture was not on his agenda. He knew so many people couldn't wait to retire, but he didn't feel like that. He liked to feel needed, and Elaine didn't need him in the same way the school needed him – if she *needed* him at all.

'No, it's all right, Jacob. But do you mind me asking who you overheard? I won't say anything, I promise.'

The colour rose even higher in Jacob's cheeks and he cleared his throat before saying, 'It was actually something Elaine said to Tabitha the other day when she was in the café picking up some cupcakes.'

Paul could see he was having difficulty continuing, so he said, 'Go on.'

Jacob glanced around. Perhaps he was worried Elaine would overhear. 'She said she was looking forward to you retiring next year, because then you could start going on back-to-back cruises like you'd always planned. She had brochures with her and everything.'

Paul sighed. 'Thanks for telling me, Jacob. Don't worry, I won't say you mentioned it.' He knew Elaine could hold a grudge if she felt anyone had dropped her in it. But what on earth was she thinking telling everyone he was retiring? What would the school think? Having told them he wanted to remain after retirement age, if they got wind of what Elaine was saying, it could put the kybosh on him staying. He'd have to have words with her; it wouldn't be a pleasant conversation, but there was no way around it.

Assuring Jacob once again that he hadn't put his foot in it, he paid for his cakes and with a heavy heart, he headed back to his office – right now, he needed to eat one of his cakes to ready him for the task ahead.

Chapter Three

'Right, class, line up,' said Bella. 'Coats and jackets on, please. It's cold outside today.' It wasn't half; she'd had to scrape her windscreen this morning. She was pretty sure Ryan had her scraper in his car, as she'd had to make do with a CD cover – one of her friends had advised her of that failsafe one day after they'd been caught short in a blizzard with no scraper. Despite the fact Bella wasn't of the CD generation, she'd dutifully borrowed one of her mum's and kept it in the car for emergencies. She'd been glad of it this morning, although the hard frost hadn't exactly made it an easy job. On the positive side, as she drove to work she'd noted how pretty everything looked, with the fields covered in a light dusting of snow and the snow-topped roofs and chimneys making it appear as if Christmas was ever nearer. Pity then that her Christmas spirit had deserted her round about the same time as her divorce papers landed.

She gave herself a little shake. With only fifteen minutes of playtime, she was dying for a coffee and for a second to collar Amy to get some advice. What she'd do without Amy, she didn't know. She was more than a best friend, more than a confidante – she was a keeper of secrets and a bringer of cheerfulness, and right now Bella needed the latter, by the bucketload.

She knew that her class, and indeed the teaching staff, viewed her as the Disney princess who was always happy, and she did always try to embrace the good things in life, not dwell on the negatives. She was, naturally, an upbeat kind of person, but there was only so much even an upbeat, glass half-full person could take before even they succumbed to negativity and ended up at a low ebb. Getting divorced less than two years from getting married was one of those things.

'Mrs Hopkins?' a voice broke into Bella's thoughts. 'Have you seen my coat?'

Bella started. She had assumed all of the children had gone out to the playground when the bell rang for playtime. But here was Lara standing in front of her.

'Sorry, Lara, I was daydreaming. What's that about your coat?'

'It's not on its peg.'

'Oh! Well, why don't we look for it together?' Pushing thoughts of warm coffee aside for a second, Bella helped Lara look for her forest green parka until it popped up in the cloakroom three classes down.

'Thanks, miss. You're the best.' Lara shot her a wide, gap-toothed smile and crashed through the doors to the playground.

With a sigh and a deep breath in, Bella steeled herself and headed for the staffroom.

'There you are!' Amy held out a cup of instant coffee to Bella, and once again Bella was grateful she'd found a kindred spirit in Amy. She and Amy were avid readers – in Amy's case romantasy, in Bella's sci-fi and epic fantasy – plus they both liked netball and red velvet cupcakes. I mean, what wasn't to like? Could she have found anyone who twinned with her more than Amy if she'd tried? She didn't think so. Plus, she had a wild sense of humour, and Bella could seriously do with a large dose of it. She could always rely on Amy to help her out of a funk – and Amy could always rely on her to give her sensible relationship advice – or rather, she could, until her marriage to Ryan fell apart after less than four hundred days. Not that she was counting or anything.

'Thanks, Amy. You're a lifesaver.'

Amy frowned and lowering her voice said, 'You OK?'

With an almost imperceptible headshake, Bella said, 'Not really. Can't talk right now.'

'Why don't we get out of here for a moment?' Amy walked out of the staffroom, held the door for Bella, then she strode across to the photocopying room and once Bella was inside, closed the door.

'What's wrong?' Her voice was filled with concern.

Suddenly Bella couldn't speak. Tears filled her eyes and her chest felt tight. It was as if by articulating the words, this would all really be happening. Her divorce from Ryan, the love of her life, the man she'd met when she was twenty and expected to have lots and lots of children with – his words – would become a reality.

'Hey.' Amy rubbed Bella's arm. 'It's OK. Take your time.'

Bella sat her coffee down on the table, opened her bag and took out a manila envelope, which she then handed to Amy.

Amy eyed her quizzically then opened the envelope and slid out the papers. 'Divorce papers?'

Bella nodded. 'They arrived this morning.'

'Aw, Bella, I'm so sorry.' Amy sat her cup beside Bella's, then hugged her, and Bella cried silently into her shoulder.

'Thanks. At this rate, I might even be divorced for Christmas.' She gave a bitter laugh.

'You're joking?' Amy said, her face stricken.

'Nope. These quickie divorces can be completed in four weeks. We have no kids and no major financial issues to iron out.' Bella's voice caught on the word 'kids'. She'd thought they were guaranteed. Wasn't that one of the main reasons they'd got married? To have a family whilst they were still in their twenties?

'Bella, don't you think you should tell some of the other staff, though? It's too much taking all this on yourself without anyone realising what you're going through.'

Bella shook her head. 'I can't face it. They were all at our wedding a little over a year ago. It's embarrassing. I've even considered giving back the gifts.'

'No one would care about that.'

'I can't cope with everyone knowing my business. I know they all think I'm Miss Sweetness and Light, but I'm finding it really hard to live up to my reputation right now.'

The bell rang and Bella exhaled loudly. 'And now I have to go back in and be that bright and breezy teacher the kids love.'

'Well, Bella, I'm here for you. You know that. And after school, we're going to Sugar and Spice to have a proper catch-up.'

Bella was about to protest. She didn't want to eat into Amy's time with her husband, but Amy wasn't having any of it.

She wagged a finger at Bella. 'Uh-uh, I'm not taking no

for an answer. Jacob's cakes may not fix everything in life, but they do go a long way.'

Bella smiled. 'Thanks, Amy, for everything.' She rested her head on her friend's shoulder then opened the photocopier room door and ran straight into Mr McCafferty, the new head. *Great.*

With a look that could have frozen yoghurt, he said, 'Mrs Hopkins. Mrs Dalwood. Can we get these children inside, please? It's rather chilly outside. We don't want them catching pneumonia, do we?'

Fraser watched the two women walk away and berated himself. He could have handled that so much better. Why did he seem to rub everyone up the wrong way? He didn't mean to, but it was happening more and more often at the moment, and he couldn't help it. No matter what he said, it came out the wrong way. He knew Paul, the janitor, hadn't been overly impressed with his comments about how he'd set out the chairs for parents' evening last week.

Fraser had been looking forward to his first Christmas as head, at his 'own' school – OK, he was only covering maternity leave – but now he couldn't wait for this term and the whole Christmas shebang to be over.

He'd be spending it alone. It had been two years since his last serious relationship ended, but at least he'd always been able to spend some quality time with his mum and his friends at the holidays. Now, his mum was in a care home. He couldn't work and look after his mum and he'd had to face facts when her persistent falls had meant she couldn't be left unsupervised for long periods of time.

Deciding he couldn't face the staffroom, he turned

back to his office. He needed to start interacting better with his staff, although right now he had too many things on his plate. He knew his guilt about putting his mother in a care home was affecting his job, but he had other issues to sort too – school-related ones – and he didn't have any more headspace right now. Not for a jolly Santa Claus, or a frosted snowman or a googly-eyed reindeer. How he wished he did, but right now, his focus had to be on two areas and two areas only. He'd have to leave the joyful, cheerful stuff to his staff team. If only he could go into hibernation and come out in January, he'd be much happier.

Chapter Four

'Ivy, sweetie, can you hold the door for me, please?' said Valerie, trying to manoeuvre the double pram through the door of Sugar and Spice.

When Tabitha had messaged Valerie earlier to ask if she fancied a catch-up at the café, she'd jumped at the chance. She had no idea what she'd have done without Tabitha's friendship. Even the possibility to hand off one of the twins to another human being who didn't moan about it, whilst she nursed the other, was a godsend.

She breathed a sigh of relief when she saw Tabitha had already reserved them a table, and that it had both space for the pram beside it and it was next to a book corner Jacob had installed recently. She could murder a cinnamon latte, but she'd wait to see what festive delights Jacob had come up with this year.

An added bonus to having Tabitha as a best friend was the fact she co-owned Sugar and Spice with her brother, Jacob. And the icing on the cake was Tabitha had her own Etsy shop, and pretty much kept her own hours, so was often available for a chat. As Valerie waved to her friend, who plumped up the cushions on the low sofa where she preferred to sit, a rare wave of contentment swept over her. She had no idea having twins at forty-three would addle her brain and leave her constantly assailed by feelings of guilt. Guilt that she wasn't producing enough milk; guilt that she was neglecting Ivy, even though she didn't mean to. Therefore, it was balm to her soul to see another human who'd been through a tough time of it when they'd had children, or in Tabitha's case, a child. Since Lara's father had never been on the scene, Tabitha had brought Lara up on her own, and Valerie thought that was also why she got on so well with Tabitha – she admired her. In many ways, she reminded her of her younger self. Hungry to succeed. Yet at the same time, by Tabitha's own admission, she'd downsized – traded one business for another, found her niche in making intricate, gorgeous jewellery, which she sold via her Etsy shop and at exclusive craft fairs. The school fair she did as a favour. Whatever – Tabitha had the right idea.

As Valerie greeted her friend, and Ivy joined Lara in the adjacent book corner, she pushed to the back of her mind her boss' emails asking when she'd be returning to work.

'Hi! Wow, you guys have been busy,' Valerie said, sitting down and casting her eyes around the café and the bakery. 'This is gorgeous.'

'You know Jacob likes to go large when it comes to Christmas.' Tabitha lifted Noah out of the pram and held him against her. 'Oh, I'd forgotten how amazing he smells.'

'Not all the time, he doesn't,' said Ivy. 'Keep away from the other end.'

Tabitha laughed and Valerie's eyes lingered on her elder daughter. Elder. She was still getting used to the idea. Going from one child to three had been such a shock, and she wasn't sure she was getting used to it as well as she'd hoped. She was certainly an awful lot more tired than she'd anticipated.

As she levered Poppy out of her pram and cradled her against her, she realised she'd had this overly rose-tinted ideal of being a mum to twins. Foolishly, Valerie thought her husband, Munro, would pitch in and lend a hand when they had three children, yet despite her being an interpreter with a major oil company, and making pretty good money, he didn't seem to have received the memo that he needed to up his game and get out of bed in the middle of the night and help with the twins. Yes, he worked hard, really hard, and he had a responsible job, with lots of people counting on him, and he provided well for their family, but so did she. Now, exhausted, Valerie was juggling all the balls and too many were cascading down around her.

Jacob came over. 'Hi, Valerie. Hands full?'

She rolled her eyes. 'Hi, Jacob. Plate's full too, metaphorically speaking.'

'Can I hold her a sec?' he asked, eyeing Poppy, who had her eyes closed, perfect thick eyelashes lying against her cheeks as if she were in an advert for a most gorgeous baby competition.

'Sure.' Valerie passed her precious bundle to Jacob, who held her tenderly against him.

He'd make a great dad, she thought. Absent-mindedly she wondered why Sophie and Jacob didn't have kids yet. She knew they'd been together since before Lara was born. She didn't want to pry, but she hoped their lack of kids wasn't because they couldn't have them. Studying him, the way he held Poppy, in one hand, cradled against him, he looked a natural.

She couldn't help her resentment at Munro from kicking in. Although she loved all of her children, she'd have been happy to stick at one – as she adored Ivy – but

Munro had talked her round, and she *was* delighted she had the twins. She was a little less delighted that the lion's share of caring for them fell on her shoulders – and she didn't mean the feeding part; that was a given. She meant the constant washing; the buying of baby products and clothes; taking them for immunisations, whatever. It all fell to her, as well as helping Ivy with her schoolwork, taking her to classes after school, play dates – although that was a blessing in disguise if they were with Lara and Tabitha. However, it was never-ending and she was drained.

Couldn't Munro see she needed a rest? And then – and at this she almost laughed out loud hysterically – he had the nerve to ask what she was buying his parents from them for Christmas. That so wasn't her responsibility! Surely no one could be that blind.

The café wasn't particularly busy right then and Jacob wandered over to the bakery with Poppy.

'He loves babies,' said Tabitha. 'He was really good with Lara. Still is. Plus, she absolutely adores him.'

'I know. He could teach some men a thing or two,' Valerie said.

When Tabitha raised an eyebrow, Valerie said, 'Sorry. I'm feeling a bit harassed at the moment.'

'And underappreciated?' Tabitha asked.

Valerie sighed and examined her nails, which were badly in need of a manicure. 'Is it that obvious?'

'Just a tad. Listen, sometimes you need to tell it to them straight.' She paused then said, 'Leave him instructions on the fridge. I used to do that with Jacob. Believe me, he's not perfect, my brother. When I was living with him, when I was pregnant, he was wonderful, but eventually some of his habits got on my nerves, and I had to tell him, as he was o-bliv-i-ous.'

'I can relate to that.' Valerie's eyes wandered to the bakery where some of the patrons were making a fuss of a still sleeping Poppy. 'Although I simply can't imagine Jacob being as unaware as Munro. With Munro it's as if, if something doesn't affect him directly, he doesn't need to deal with it.' She stopped then sighed. She didn't want to be disloyal to her husband, but she was so thoroughly fed up and overwhelmed. 'Anyway, what has been happening with you? How did the Christmas fair go?'

Tabitha's eyes lit up as she spoke of how complimentary everyone had been and how she'd been astonished by the number of sales she'd made.

'That's incredible. Well done, you. I wish I was crafty, but my only creativity comes through in the languages I speak,' said Valerie, her mouth turning down at the corners slightly.

'I'm sure that's not true,' said Tabitha.

'Oh, no, I assure you it is. Ask me to talk about the inner workings of a car engine in Japanese, or discuss jet propulsion with an aerospace engineer, and I'm fine. Ask me to crochet or make anything out of papier mâché, or anything that requires any level of practicality, and I am so not your person for it.'

Tabitha laughed. 'Well, we'll just have to get you involved in our Christmas craft night here at the café.'

Ivy, who had been eavesdropping, piped up, 'There's a Christmas craft night? Mummy, please say we can come,' as Tabitha's brows knitted and she mouthed sorry to Valerie.

Valerie turned to Ivy. 'Depends when it is, sweetie.'

Ivy looked to Tabitha, who said, 'Next Tuesday at six o'clock.'

Valerie tried to work out if the kids, and by extension she, had anything else on that day. She gave a sigh of resignation. 'That should be OK.'

'Yay.' Ivy clapped her hands together. 'Lara, did you hear that? We're coming to the craft night.'

Lara looked at Valerie and smiled. Valerie liked Lara, a lot. She was a sweet little girl and a great influence on Ivy, and her calming presence meant Valerie didn't feel such a failure of a mother when Lara was around to entertain Ivy. That very thought gave her another pang of guilt.

'Great, that's all settled then,' Valerie said, a little overbrightly. Despite being delighted it would be another evening Ivy would have company that wasn't her own – since she felt lacking in that department at the moment – the familiar sensation of panic assailed her at the thought of yet another event booked into the calendar at such an incredibly busy time of year. She'd already pencilled in the *Jolabokaflod* for Christmas Eve with Lara, as Ivy had made her promise to take her to T&J's to buy a book for Lara, so they could exchange at the read-in.

Valerie tried surreptitiously to take the deep, calming breaths her meditation app told her to, but almost laughed out loud – meditation app. She'd downloaded it, listened to ninety seconds of it before one of the twins had woken up screaming the place down, and about three minutes before Ivy had fallen down the stairs. Valerie had rocked one child in one arm, whilst trying to simultaneously comfort her elder daughter and clean up a scrape and apply a plaster. Tricky wasn't the word.

'Tabitha, please, tell me more about your life. The good stuff. I need it. Sorry if that's selfish, but I do, plus you all too often have to listen to me drone on about being sicked up on, or having run out of nappies, or not having slept at all. It's so uninteresting, and you've weathered the storm admirably. So…' Valerie placed her hands in her lap '…anything new to tell me?'

Tabitha made a face. 'If you mean on the dating front, then no. And because you have to actively go out and "put yourself out there", that's not likely to happen. Believe me, I've done the rock 'n' roll lifestyle. I don't need it any more. I have Lara, and Tabitha's Trinkets, and this.' She threw her hands wide to encompass Sugar and Spice. 'And I get to enjoy plenty of family time, both with Lara, and my brother and sister-in-law. I have enough family. I don't need anyone else, and I don't need a relationship.'

'Oh, Tabitha, I know you don't *need* anyone, but don't you *want* someone? I mean, there's a limit to how much Netflix you can watch after Lara's gone to bed, and making jewellery until after midnight isn't exactly the most social of pursuits.'

'I know, but I'm happy, and, well, I don't want to upset the dynamic at home with Lara. We have a very special relationship, since it has always been only the two of us – well, apart from Sophie and Jacob – and I wouldn't want to spoil that.'

'Hmm.' Valerie was unconvinced. If she truly thought Tabitha was done with love and didn't hanker after it, she wouldn't insist, but she had this gut feeling Tabitha really would like to have someone to share her life with, but either didn't know how to go about it, or was simply putting her child first. Most mums did that, she thought wryly. At the end of the day, though, Tabitha deserved a life of her own, too, and not solely one that revolved around work and family.

Whilst Valerie was frustrated by her husband's inability to intuit her need for help with the kids and the house, she wouldn't be without him for the world. At forty-five, he was even better-looking now than when they'd met fifteen years earlier, and they'd had the first few years getting to know each other, just being together, without the added complication of children. From what Tabitha had told her, she'd never had that – never had a serious relationship since she'd had Lara. But Valerie wondered if she'd had *any* relationships since Lara was born.

If Munro's colleagues weren't complete dullards, she'd have proposed one of them, but she'd met far too many of them at the company events Munro dragged her to, to foist them on Tabitha.

After Jacob brought Poppy back over and Valerie settled both twins in the pram, she dearly wished she could help her friend. Tabitha deserved love in her life – they all did.

Chapter Five

'Mr Fairbairn, could you help Mrs Hopkins and Mrs Dalwood move some of the sets after rehearsals, please? As you know, I have a presentation to give to parents that I need to use the games hall for.'

'Of course, Mr McCafferty.'

As the head wandered off towards the playground, Paul shook his head. He couldn't work out why the man was always so formal with everyone. Every other member of staff in the building called each other by their first name. It wasn't as if Fraser McCafferty was old either; he was only late thirties, early forties perhaps. Young enough to be his son, in fact. Paul sighed, recalling how his son, James, had moved to Canberra fifteen years earlier, and only returned twice. Sure, it had given him a good reason to travel there himself, three times thus far, but Australia wasn't for him. It was gorgeous, although too vast, and he could have done without that trip into the Bush, where deadly snakes lurked at every corner. No, thank you. He'd rather go on a cruise around Loch Katrine or to Loch Lomond.

Paul wasn't sure what it was about Fraser McCafferty, but he sensed everything about the man was a façade, and since he didn't open himself up to anyone, how could they get to know the real him? He was snappish and grumpy with his staff. He was better with the kids, although he wasn't exactly warm with them either – like he wasn't really in his natural habitat. Did he feel out of his depth?

He'd had big shoes to fill as the previous head had been much beloved and pretty much everyone had shed a tear when she went on maternity leave. At this rate, no one would be able to say the same about Fraser when he left. And who knew how long they were stuck with him for. He was on secondment, which everyone knew was code for 'here on a temporary basis, but could be extended'. What happened if Mrs Russell decided not to come back after her maternity leave ended? Maybe she'd decide, as an older mum, that she'd like to spend more time with her child.

As the only other man in the school, Paul had had high hopes of enjoying at least a little bit of camaraderie with Fraser. He considered himself an open and friendly person, and he knew he was popular with parents and pupils alike. He wasn't being big-headed; it was simply a fact that he made a point of ensuring all the children and their parents felt welcome at the school. He loved his job, and he was pretty sure it showed. Often he'd lock up late or go to open up the school gate early in order to chew the fat with some of the parents. He saw that as part of his janitorial role, too.

Hearing the children in full flow in their nativity play rehearsal, he sneaked in at the back and sat for a few moments, drinking in the atmosphere. Christmas was his favourite time of year, and he especially enjoyed all the school events.

He smiled fondly as little Becky Richmond forgot her lines – she was a donkey and only had two lines. Wee sweetheart. He had a lump in his throat as her eyes filled with tears and she started bawling. Bella went to comfort her. He wondered where the primary one teacher was. Maybe he should offer to take Becky back to class if she was so upset, as Bella and Amy were busy running through the show with all the children. Five donkeys, four wise men – he wasn't sure when they did their maths, but last time he checked there were three wise men. Maybe one was an understudy. They'd been caught out the year before, when the morning of the nativity, the boy playing Joseph had gone down with chickenpox, and a brave Hamish McGuiness had stood up and volunteered to play Joseph instead. Paul had been watching him mouthing the words from the sidelines for two weeks. He knew Hamish was word perfect and he was pleased the boy had had the chance to perform and to shine.

As the children sang the carols, particularly 'We Three Kings', then followed that by a rap version called 'No Danger', whose tune bore a striking similarity to 'Away in a Manger', Paul sat back and listened, fully taking in the magic, the stuttered lines, the missteps, and he revelled in it all. Being a part, however small, of a child's formative years was a gift to him. He knew some significant fact about every one of the children in the school, all two hundred and forty-seven of them; whether it was their favourite cartoon, pop star, something about their hobby – everything from handball to creating unicorn mosaics – it was almost like his specialist subject. Maybe he should apply to *Mastermind*. He hid a smile at the thought; he didn't think the viewing public were up to that.

Basically, he cared. He watched these children grow, sometimes from little tots; sometimes he met them for the first time when they were still in their mums' bellies, and sometimes they weren't even a twinkling in their parents' eyes yet, particularly when he considered how many parents had also gone to school here as children whilst he was janitor.

Of course, many people had moved away, often to look for work, or to pursue interests elsewhere, but quite a few former pupils had stayed in the town. Winstanton had that hold on you. It was a lovely place to live, and an even lovelier place to bring up children.

Paul started at the sound of Bella's voice, as she guided Bethany Watson to the position on the stage, to the right of the crib, where she and 'Joseph' would sit on the straw. Then he choked as Leo Tiernan tried to ad lib his lines and work a mobile phone into the birth of Jesus. Paul loved how every year was different, how every show was different, and how every year there were different kids whose antics – sometimes intentional, other times not so intentional – made him laugh so much he had tears streaming down his face.

As the bell rang for break and Bella and Amy shepherded the children out to the playground, his one thought was *I'm not ready to retire yet – not by a long chalk.*

Valerie hated how not long after she returned from picking up Ivy from school, twins in tow, soaking wet from the torrential rain that had been lashing down all day, it was already dark. It wasn't even four o'clock yet. Not that it had been very bright in the first place. A bit like her mood.

She hadn't had the best start to the day. Of course, she'd been in a rush, and had gone to plop the twins in their car seats in order to drop Ivy at school, and found the car seat bases missing. She'd vaguely remembered Munro switching them over to his car at the weekend when he took them to visit his folks. He'd wanted her to go with him, but honestly, she'd needed a sleep. She reckoned her cumulative sleep for the week was around twelve hours. No wonder she looked like the living dead and the great unwashed. She'd gone for a long bath, during which she'd almost fallen asleep, then dragged herself out of it and into bed, to grab a blissful two hours of uninterrupted sleep. Exhaustion could be handy sometimes.

She didn't have bags under her eyes, she had Santa sacks ... but without the presents. She yawned. That was all she seemed to do these days, too – yawn. She didn't remember it being this hard when she had Ivy. Sure, Ivy was only one baby, rather than two at once, but everyone had told her right up until the twins' birth that two babies weren't actually twice as much work. Liars. And Ivy was so sweet with Noah and Poppy. She loved babies and was forever cuddling her new siblings. They'd be two months old in a few days.

On top of her boss already hassling her to come back early from mat leave – she didn't think legally he was allowed to pester her in this way, although since when had that ever stopped anyone? – her husband seemed to have forgotten the promise they'd made that they would always be equal partners in their work and family lives.

The minute his paternity leave was over, all two weeks of it, he'd made barely any effort. Yes, he came in to check on the twins when he returned from work – probably to see if they'd changed any since he left – but that was the extent of his involvement. He'd always thought newborns were boring – didn't think children were exciting until they were much older. Well, Ivy, at nine, should definitely meet that prerequisite, and whilst he was happy to interact with her, watching TV together, doing a little of her homework with her and discussing what she'd asked Santa for, he didn't seem to think doing his bit with the twins or the housework was in his remit.

This morning, when she'd found the Isofix bases for the car seats missing, she had wanted to scream. Where had he put them? Why hadn't he put them back in the car? They weren't in the hallway. Taking Poppy back inside in her car seat, Valerie had set her down in the hall and gone looking for the bases. Finally, she'd found them in the garage. By the time she'd put them back in the car, closed the garage, retrieved Poppy, then Noah and told Ivy to get in the car, they were late for school.

Didn't Munro realise how supposedly little actions had far-reaching consequences when you had not one but two newborns, another child and a time by which you had to be somewhere? She was still fuming at his thoughtlessness as she unloaded the washing machine hours later.

'Mum, can I have hot chocolate, please?'

Valerie started as Ivy interrupted her flow. She could unload and reload a washing machine with the same speed a Formula One race team could change a tyre, and she had to, given how much washing there was – all the tiny vests, muslin squares and bibs, babygros, not to mention Ivy's school uniform and sports kit for her various classes, both at school and outside.

'Sure, sweetheart. Just give me a minute. Can you bring me down the white laundry basket, the one I use for storing ironing? I think it's in the spare room. If not, it might be in my bedroom.'

'No problem. And Mum, can we write my letter to

Santa after we have our hot chocolate?'

Valerie smiled. 'Absolutely.'

'Yay!' Ivy dashed off as Valerie thought how sweet and helpful her elder daughter was. She had been a godsend since the twins came, but Valerie hated making her daughter her own personal gopher; she was only a kid herself. No, Valerie needed Munro to realise he was the one who should be supporting her. She couldn't remember the last time he'd put the washing on, but he expected all his clothes to be washed and ironed ready for work.

He might be a hotshot CEO at his company, Dynamic Innovation Inc., but that didn't cut the mustard when he was at home. Sure, he was making about fifty grand more than she was, but she'd put opening her own interpreting and translation company on hold when they'd decided to have Ivy. Valerie had made sacrifices, whereas she didn't feel Munro had, and although she wouldn't turn back the clock for anything, a little more support would help greatly and perhaps put her building feelings of resentment towards her husband back in a box.

'Here you go, Mum.' Ivy held out the laundry basket and Valerie leant forward and kissed her on the head.

'Thank you. Right, you know the drill. Grab the marshmallows, a mug and the milk, and I'll be back in three minutes, tops. I just need to hang up this washing.'

'OK.' Ivy bounced away from the worktop and started opening cupboards to line up all the ingredients.

As she edged open the kitchen door with her elbow, Valerie glanced at her daughter and smiled to see her long blonde plaits swinging to and fro as she set to her task. Ivy was such a good kid. She needed to spend more time with her. Before the twins arrived she'd been so tired – being pregnant with twins was a totally different ballgame to being pregnant with one, in much the same way as having two newborns was different to having only one. And now, she had her hands full – literally, at the moment – with the twins and housework and life stuff, and if her boss didn't stop calling her, asking when she was coming back, she would go to HR. Surely there were laws to protect her from this level of harassment.

She tiptoed upstairs. The twins were sleeping, thankfully. She began hanging up the washing – they really needed to get the tumble dryer fixed. She'd forgotten how reliant she'd been on one when Ivy was a newborn, and as a family of three they'd been able to cope with drying the washing outside – but not in winter – or on airers in the spare room, and when you had as much washing as newborns produced, that simply wasn't an option. As she pegged the final yellow bib to the airer, a wail from the twins' room made her groan.

Oh no! All I want to do is have a mug of hot chocolate with my girl. Is that too much to ask?

She wondered if it was Poppy or Noah. Poppy had been more fractious than her brother this afternoon certainly, but Valerie had fully expected them to sleep at least another half an hour. Making her way down the hallway to the twins' bedroom, she banged her leg on a large plastic box.

I'm going to kill Munro. Bloody Christmas decorations. She'd told him to pick up the tree two days before. Of course, he hadn't, and she'd gone to the hassle of getting the decorations out of the loft as Ivy was desperate to dress the tree. She'd been in Sugar and Spice at the end of November and been raving about how amazing their tree looked and all the special and unusual baubles on it. Valerie had seen it for herself yesterday and even jogged Munro's memory regarding picking up the tree, but still no tree when he returned yesterday – he'd been caught up late in a meeting. He had to start stepping up – he couldn't keep putting them last. Ivy's eyes had dulled when he'd told them he hadn't managed to pick up a tree and Valerie had balled her hands into fists to prevent herself throwing the first thing to hand at her husband. How could he be so oblivious?

She reached into Poppy's Moses basket, trying to comfort her without lifting her, praying her baby daughter would go back to sleep so she wouldn't have to renege on her plans with Ivy. The poor little thing had been neglected enough of late, and she hated to feel she was inadvertently pushing her aside, but unfortunately the twins physically needed her more at the moment, and there was only so much of her to go around.

Her long black hair caught Poppy's attention and soon Valerie was engaged in a battle of wits to disentangle her hair. No sooner had she gained some ground than Poppy grabbed hold of another section, and Valerie was ever mindful of Noah in the next basket to his sister, and implored a higher authority to let him continue to sleep.

The door behind her creaked open and Ivy's anxious little face appeared. Valerie mouthed 'Sorry,' then 'Just a minute.'

Ivy gave a resigned smile then retreated.

Valerie sighed inwardly then gently rocked the Moses basket in a desperate attempt to lull Poppy back to sleep. Three minutes passed. Four. Five. She was beginning to despair her younger daughter would never fall asleep and her elder would be left alone – again – when finally Poppy's eyes drifted closed.

Hallelujah. Valerie waited another one or two minutes, to be sure, then quietly tiptoed out of the room, leaving the room door slightly ajar to avoid it creaking again.

She popped her head into the living room where Ivy was watching *Nativity 3: Dude, Where's My Donkey?*, a favourite of hers. Personally, Valerie preferred the original, but she was happy to watch that one too.

'Ivy, Poppy's asleep. Hot chocolate?'

Ivy jumped up, then hit pause on the remote control. 'Yes, please, with extra marshmallows.'

Valerie pulled her daughter into a hug. 'Ivy Nicol, I love you. Don't ever change.'

'I love you, too, Mum.' Ivy grinned. 'Now, can I have whipped cream with the hot chocolate too?'

'Sounds like a plan.'

As they prepared the hot chocolate together, Ivy told Valerie everything she'd like to include on her Santa list. None of the items were particularly expensive – no laptops or games consoles or smart watches or anything. Ivy wanted roller blades. Apparently, they were back in vogue; she'd seen a pair on TV – in black and green – and those were the ones she wanted. Next on her list were a table tennis table and some books she'd noted down last time they were in a bookshop – prior to the twins' arrival. The final item she'd asked for was a musical jump rope machine.

'This may be a stupid question, Ivy, but what is that exactly?'

Ivy rolled her eyes. 'You really don't know?'

'Well, no. I've never heard of it before. Can you show me?'

Ivy retrieved her iPad and sat down beside her.

As Valerie looked at her, really looked at her, her breath caught. When had Ivy grown so much? Her school jumper was a little on the short side, and she could tell that the pinafore was a good few centimetres short too. After they'd finished this list, she'd need to log on and order her a few new clothes. She couldn't wait until Christmas. When had she taken such a stretch? *Probably when you were busy popping out twins*, her inner voice told her.

'Mum, watch the video.' Ivy held out the iPad for Valerie to see.

When it finished two minutes later, Valerie said, 'So it's not just a clever name, it really is a musical automatic skipping rope.'

Ivy nodded. 'Yep.'

'But why do you need an automatic one? Won't your friends play real jump rope with you?'

Ivy sighed and looked at Valerie wistfully. 'Well, sometimes Lara and I play with the other kids at school, but at home, there's no one for me to play with, and you and Dad are too busy.'

Valerie bit her lip to stop herself from crying. She needed to find some more time to spend with Ivy, but how?

Chapter Six

'Ryan, what are you doing here?' Bella said as she locked her car with the key fob, then had to open it again to get her house keys out of the tray next to the gearstick. To say she was flustered at arriving home to find her husband on their doorstep only days after she'd received divorce papers would have been an understatement.

'It is still my house, you know,' Ryan replied, his jaw set, his eyes flashing.

Bella had no idea why he was always so angry now. She couldn't think of a single thing she'd done that would cause him to act this way towards her.

'You know that's not what I meant. I wasn't expecting you, that's all.'

'Yes, well, I wanted to know if you'd received my package.'

Bella's heart sank. She'd had a good day, or as good a day as you can have when you've just received divorce papers and your head is spinning, but the nativity rehearsals had been fun, and she'd left school feeling a little bit positive, for the first time in a while, or rather, since Ryan had left.

'If you mean the divorce papers, yes.'

Ryan stood over her. 'So, can we get them signed then?

Maybe make a fresh start in the New Year?'

It took Bella a few moments to realise that his fresh start didn't include her, even though he'd said 'we'.

'Ryan, it's a big step, and I've only just received them. I haven't even read them yet.'

'What?' Ryan shook his head. 'You're kidding, right?'

The beginnings of a headache were making themselves known to Bella. She touched her right hand to her temple and gently massaged it with her fingers.

'No, Ryan, I'm not kidding. Believe it or not, I do have other things to do, other commitments. I dare say a couple of days won't make any difference. Now, if you'll excuse me, I have marking to do.'

'Rock 'n' roll, eh?' Ryan said.

Bella, key half inserted in the door, spun around. 'What's that supposed to mean?'

'Oh, c'mon, Belles, we used to do stuff, go places. Now you're always "busy marking".'

'Ryan, it's my job. I have to mark the kids' assignments. And it's not as if I spend every waking hour marking, is it? No more than you spend playing rugby or squash or whatever other sports you indulge in after work.'

'Actually, that's one of the reasons why I'm here. My spare squash racquet is in the loft and I broke the strings on the other one. It's quicker and easier to get the spare than go into town and have my good one restrung.'

Bella stared at her husband. Was he really so insensitive? Couldn't he see how much his being here upset her, and all for a squash racquet? Days after he served divorce papers on her?

Bella could feel anger build up from somewhere deep inside her. How could he? Tears weren't far away and she did not under any circumstances want to cry in front of him. She wouldn't give him the satisfaction.

'Fine. Come in and get your racquet. You can let yourself out.'

For a moment, something flickered in his eyes. Sorrow? Regret? She'd probably imagined it, like she'd imagined he loved her. She often wondered now if she'd dreamt the whole thing – their love affair. Surely it wasn't possible to fall in love and out again so readily? Although, clearly, it had been for Ryan.

Back ramrod straight, she marched into the house, switched the lights on and dumped her handbag on the kitchen counter, as their spaniel, Mac, went berserk at Ryan's presence. She flicked the kettle on for tea – for her; she wasn't offering him a cup. He could go to hell. Honestly, she fancied a glass of wine, but that was a dangerous road to start down. She wasn't someone who held grudges or harboured resentment, and she hated feeling this way, but it was hard to be cheerful when this was her reality.

To give him his due, Ryan didn't follow her into the kitchen; instead, once he'd fussed over Mac, she heard him thump up the stairs, towards the loft, presumably. She heaved a sigh of relief and set a cup out for tea, then she leant her elbows on the worktop and put her head in her hands. Would she ever feel better? Happier? For now it was as though her technicolour world had been pared back to a sepia-tinted shadow of its former self.

She couldn't even really go out with a friend, as she hadn't told anyone except Amy that she and Ryan had split up. She realised now she'd been holding on to the hope of a reconciliation – everyone said they were perfect for each other. Everything had kicked off when she'd raised the matter of having children; they'd always wanted children. He'd been stressed at work, or she'd assumed that was the reason behind his initial bad moods and snappishness, but when she'd pressed him, he'd closed her down, and when she'd persisted, he'd picked up his car keys and gone for a drive. He never did tell her where he went or what was going on in his head.

She was sipping her tea and had sat down at their walnut two-person bistro table in the kitchen, Mac now curled at her feet, when Ryan reappeared.

'Got it!' He held the racquet aloft as if he were celebrating an Olympic victory.

Bully for you, thought Bella. Out loud, she said, 'Great,' and returned her attention to the scintillating blank table. She hadn't even had the foresight to take out her marking to pretend she was engrossed in doing something and couldn't stop.

'I'll be off then.'

'OK.'

She sensed him hover near the door, possibly unsure how to take her abrupt reply. Then she heard his steps heading off down the hall and she exhaled a long, low breath. She'd just about collected herself when she realised she hadn't heard the door close.

He must have soft-closed it. I'd better lock up.

As she walked into the hall, Ryan barrelled into her from the living room and she screamed, her heart thumping, and Mac started barking as if an intruder had broken in.

Ryan rested his hands on her arms. 'Sorry, I didn't mean to frighten you.'

Bella flinched as if his touch had scorched her skin. It was the first time he'd touched her since he left, and a whole host of memories – mainly good – shot through her synapses like lottery balls going round and round awaiting selection.

Their first kiss on the steps of the theatre after he'd taken her to see *Mamma Mia*. The day they moved into this house, and their removal truck hadn't turned up – they'd slept on bean bags they'd mooched from a friend, and ordered Chinese takeaway from what had become their favourite restaurant in the area. She still remembered how much they'd laughed as they'd stood against the kitchen worktop, feeding each other spring rolls and joking how this wasn't how it happened in the movies.

Their wedding, where Ryan had looked into her eyes with such sincerity and told her he couldn't imagine ever being happier, and told her how much he loved her. She felt their souls had connected that day, on some deeper level. She had really bought into a long-term future with him, and she was convinced, on that day, he'd believed it too. No one could lie so effectively. And why would they?

She recalled how the registrar had mixed up their names, calling him Ryan Ryder and her Bella Hopkins, when she was still Bella Ryder, and he'd always been Ryan Hopkins. The registrar had turned the colour of the angry emoji and looked mortified. They'd all laughed about it afterwards, of course.

And then there was last Christmas, where they had lain in bed until late, then finally got up and had scrambled eggs and avocado on toast as they opened their gifts. Ryan had presented her with a white gold eternity ring with tiny diamonds on the inside, and she'd given him a chronograph watch he'd been coveting.

Standing opposite her in the hallway, Ryan retracted his hands as if he'd been clawed by a cat, and when Bella looked up at him, his jaw was rigid and his eyes had shuttered over.

'Belles, where are all the Christmas decorations?' He glanced around at the stark interior of the house they'd chosen as their starter home. Bella bit back a bitter laugh. If only they'd known it would be their final home.

She turned towards him, her voice thick. 'Why? Do you want those too?'

For a moment, Ryan's expression softened. 'No, but you always decorate everything beautifully. You make it feel all homely. Have you not had time yet?'

Unable to believe his insensitivity, Bella said, deadpan, 'No, I've been too busy marking.'

Ryan stared at her. For a second, it seemed he may say something, but then wordlessly he opened the door and left.

Bella closed the door, then walked down the hallway to their living room.

Why were some men so stupid?

She sat on their cuddle chair, and swiped at tears spilling from her eyes as she considered the irony of its name.

How could everything have gone so wrong so quickly?

When Mac jumped up on the chair beside her, she buried her head into his lovely silky coat and wept until she had nothing left.

Chapter Seven

'Now, everyone, eyes front. Mrs Dalwood, can you start playing "O Little Town of Bethlehem" after three, please?'

Amy, who'd been trying to place each of the choir in optimal positions to play to their strengths, nodded and the iPod sprang to life, the uplifting notes of the carol making goose bumps rise on Bella's skin. She loved Christmas, and she loved Christmas carols, all of them. She always had, even as a little girl. Her favourite was 'Silent Night' when sung by someone who really knew how to sing. It could be a catastrophe otherwise, as she'd found out the previous year when Rio in her primary six class had decided he should sing it for the solo. She wasn't sure her ears had ever recovered.

Bella's heart lifted. The kids had been practising their little hearts out for A Carol for Christmas, where the children from Heatherwood and the five neighbouring primary schools took part in a sing-off to see which school choir would be crowned the area's champion. They were singing so well, together, but she still didn't have anyone to sing the solo. No one voice out of the whole choir, or at least those who had volunteered to do it, seemed able to cope with it.

Perhaps she and Amy should rethink the solo. 'O Holy

Night' was, after all, widely known as a difficult carol to sing for a soloist, with the breadth of vocal range involved and those high notes to hit.

As she listened to the children's sweet voices singing 'O Little Town of Bethlehem', she tried to focus in on the sound of each child's voice individually.

When the carol finished, she beckoned Amy over. 'Have a drink, everyone. We're going to need those voices again in a second.'

'What's up?' Amy asked as she approached.

Bella pulled on her bottom lip as she thought. 'How about we play a little game?'

'What were you thinking?'

'Well, we're no closer to finding a soloist, and we only have two weeks until the finals, so I'm wondering if we can smoke out this soloist by having each child sing a line of a song, or a couple of lines, and see how they get on with it.'

Amy pursed her lips. 'That might just work.'

'Good. Can you think of a fun way to make this into a game for them?'

'Give me five minutes,' Amy said, walking backwards towards the stage again and holding her hands up in a double thumbs-up sign.

Once she'd got the children's attention, Amy said, 'Right, can everyone go and grab a chair and put it in the middle of the room? I need them back to back to form two rows.'

The children dashed to the left side of the room, lifting, dragging and screeching the chairs, which they and the children in the lower years had adorned with covers featuring snowmen, reindeer, snowflakes and Christmas trees as part of the school's attempt to make it the most

Christmassy year ever at Heatherwood.

Once everything was in place, Amy said, 'Right, we're going to play a game of musical chairs. If you're out, I want you to sing the next two lines in the carol. Got it?'

Fifty nodding heads later, Bella was applauding her friend on her genius. As the opening chords of 'O Come All Ye Faithful' rang out, Bella looked on whilst Amy instructed the children to walk round the chairs until the music stopped.

When it did, Eva Morrison was the first 'unlucky' child, but she took it with good grace and sang the next two lines in the carol exceptionally well. Amy restarted the process and the children giggled and chatted as time and again they had to find a seat once the music stopped.

Naturally, some jostling ensued and the occasional non-festive shove happened, but mainly the children got in the Christmas spirit and adapted.

After 'O Come All Ye Faithful', Amy played 'Silent Night' and Bella's heart faltered as Niamh Fallon sang the lines. Her voice was achingly beautiful, and suited that carol perfectly. Having decided they would indeed change the carol to 'Silent Night' and have Niamh sing it, Bella tried to signal to Amy that they were good and didn't need any more musical chairs, but Amy didn't see her, and started another round, this time with 'O Holy Night'.

As first Calum then Gregory didn't manage to hit the notes, Bella's frustration grew. *We should just knock this on the head now and let Niamh sing 'Silent Night'.*

But then Lara didn't get to a chair before Ed, and as she began to sing, a hush fell over everyone as her pure, strong, yet melodic voice floated through the games hall. Bella gulped, the hairs on her arms stood up, and she felt such a profound ache in her chest she thought she might start crying. In fact, she was crying. Oh my goodness, they'd found their soloist. Lara's voice was incredible. How had she managed to keep that hidden, and why?

Paul had been bringing a delivery of new gym equipment into the games hall when he heard the children's singing. He loved carols; he even went to church to listen to them, and he didn't really consider himself a churchgoer. But his favourite time to listen to carols was at A Carol for Christmas in the town's market square. Heatherwood had come second for the past two years, although, personally, Paul thought last year their choir should have won – not that he was biased or anything – OK, maybe just a little.

He stood and gawped at the two rows of chairs down the middle of the room. Musical chairs? Classes were certainly much more fun than in his day, but then Amy and Bella were both really good with the kids and at getting the best out of them.

When the singing stopped, he watched the children sprint round the chairs, and then vie for position to get their bums on an empty seat, to avoid being out.

He frowned when Lara, Jacob's niece and a permanent fixture at Sugar and Spice whenever he dropped in, began to sing. His skin prickled. Her singing was so heartwarming and soulful, so unexpected. He had no idea she had such a gift. She had the voice of an angel. Often you heard that term bandied about in the press, but it was true of Lara. He glanced at her fellow pupils, who sat transfixed. No one was whispering, laughing or messing about. Everyone was invested in Lara's singing. Even Aaron Park, and he could never keep quiet. He was always causing some mischief or mayhem.

Paul glanced over to where Bella was standing. Was she crying? If so, he couldn't blame her. He didn't think he'd ever heard such a beautiful voice. He honestly didn't have the words to express how it made him feel. Happy? Hopeful? Joyful? They didn't quite encompass it.

Lara turned as she hit one of the high notes and a rare ray of December sunshine flooded into the games hall, bathing her in an arc of light. She truly did look like an angel. It was incredible. OK, an angel in a grey school jumper and skirt, with a green and yellow tie, but an angel nonetheless.

As the carol finished, there was total silence, then the whole of primary six and seven clapped and then stood and gave Lara a standing ovation as her cheeks pinkened and she tried to cover her embarrassment at the attention by draping her hair over her face.

Amy stood, rooted to the spot for a second, before patting Lara on the shoulder and saying, 'Lara, that was amazing.'

Bella came over then, looked at Amy and said, 'Lara, can I have a word, please?'

Lara's face fell and Bella said, 'Don't worry. It's something good, I promise.' She led her to the side of the hall where Paul was standing and whispered, 'Lara, that was incredible. I didn't want to put you under pressure in front of everyone else, but would you sing the solo for us at A Carol for Christmas?'

Lara gulped, hesitated then slowly nodded.

'That's the spirit,' said Bella. 'Now, Mrs Dalwood will talk to you about practising for that, separate to the main choir, but first, let's go back and join your classmates. Since you sang that amazing solo, I think it's only fair you get to choose our final carol of the lesson. What would you like?'

Lara bit her lip, deep in thought, then said, '"Rudolph the Red-nosed Reindeer".'

Bella grinned. 'Done. Shall we go tell them?'

Lara nodded and Paul, catching Bella's eye as she pivoted round, smiled and gave her a thumbs-up.

It was good to see her smiling; Bella had been terribly forlorn of late, and he hadn't known how to help her. It probably wasn't something an old codger like him could help with, but he liked to try. At least Lara had put a smile on her face. And on his. He couldn't wait for A Carol for Christmas. There was no way they could lose with Lara singing the solo.

'You're joking!' Amy said as she and Bella enjoyed a quick bowl of soup down at Sugar and Spice. It was only a five-minute drive from the school and the food was so heavenly it was worth it. Definitely better to go there for lunch than have a cold sandwich brought from home and kept in a fridge all day, plus it gave them some much-needed privacy to talk.

'I'm not. He came to get his squash racquet.'

'What an insensitive–'

'Husband?'

'That's not where I was going with that.' Amy flipped her caramel-highlighted hair behind her shoulder. 'This soup is delicious.'

'I know. Jacob's carrot and parsnip is my favourite, but spiced carrot and lentil is good at this time of year, too.'

'Anyway, back to the unmentionable, AKA, idiot husband.'

'Soon to be ex-husband,' said Bella gloomily.

'I simply don't get it. You two were perfect for each other, and he was such a nice guy. What happened to make him turn into such a…?'

'I know. I have no words either. We'd talked about having kids, practically since we first met. He wanted loads of them, but all of a sudden when I suggested trying, he clammed up, then froze me out. He was like a different person.'

Amy shook her head. 'It doesn't make sense.'

As Bella sat staring into her soup, Amy said, 'Do you think he maybe came to see you for another reason, but bottled it at the last minute and talked rubbish about wanting to get his squash racquet?'

Bella sat up and looked Amy right in the eye. 'Amy, he served divorce papers on me, for goodness' sake. This isn't someone waiting for the right moment to have a heart to heart. God knows, I've tried to think of all the possibilities, the positives – haven't found any of those yet. No, what's the saying – the simplest explanation is usually the right one? Well, I think it's accurate in this case: he doesn't want to be with me.'

Bella's voice cracked and, shoulders hunched, she took some gulps of her soup to avoid crying. She had to choke it down, but she wouldn't break down, not in here. Sugar and Spice was her sanctuary.

She glanced around, taking in the chatter of other people around her – an elderly couple discussing an imminent trip to a garden centre to pick up their Christmas tree; two mums with babies in highchairs and a toddler they were trying to prevent falling off a chair; a group of girls in their mid-teens, eating cupcakes and showing each other videos on their phones.

It was hard to escape the chaos that was her life right now. Sugar and Spice's welcoming atmosphere helped a little, with its warm yellow lights suspended from the ceiling and large Christmas star lights dotted around the café adding to the cosy ambiance, not to mention the phenomenal Douglas fir with its sweet-smelling needles. However, being surrounded by so much happiness and hope also made her feel all the more hopeless, as if her situation couldn't be remedied. She was adult enough to know that, in time, things would improve and she would no longer feel the ache she felt each morning when she woke, but having to go into school and paste a smile on her face was exhausting, particularly at this time of year. Plus, naturally, she had to be on top form for the children, who came in each day, eager to find out what festive work she had planned for them.

Usually, this was her favourite part of the school year, but now it felt like a curse. Not even the children telling her the antics of their elves could raise more than a superficial smile.

'Enough of me whingeing about my less than perfect life at the moment, tell me something good about yours,' Bella said, giving her friend a rueful smile.

'Well, I'm going out for dinner next week with Dylan and a few friends. You should come.'

Bella made a face. 'Hmm, you don't want me ruining your evening with my sad face and moaning.'

'Well, don't come with a sad face then, and don't moan. You've got a week or so. Prepare. It'll be good for you, I promise.'

'Famous last words.' When Amy continued to look at her, Bella rolled her eyes. 'OK, I'll think about it.'

She would, even though it was the very last thing she felt like doing right now.

Chapter Eight

Fraser breathed a sigh of relief as he found a parking space right outside Sugar and Spice. Time was tight as he had to be back at the school in half an hour. In the afternoon, he had a meeting with the education authority for a performance review. What a time to do it, right in the middle of all the extra Christmas events.

The town centre was already busier with people bustling around during their lunch hour, trying to get ahead in buying gifts for their loved ones, no doubt. Fraser cleared his throat as a wave of emotion hit him. He couldn't cry, not here.

He felt he was letting his mum down – that was putting it mildly – but he'd had to accept the truth. She wasn't safe, and he couldn't protect her. It wasn't feasible for him to live with her – she'd told him, much as she loved him, he would drive her bonkers being with her all the time, and he'd agreed, and he didn't want to totally give up his independence either. He knew that was selfish, but he was only forty-three, and he didn't want to be known as 'that man in his forties who lives with his mum'. One day, he still hoped to have a wife and a family, although that dream seemed ever more distant.

For now, as he braced himself for yet another visit to

Bay Park Care Home, all he could do was ensure she was comfortable and had as many of her favourite things and treats as he could buy her. However, sometimes he felt as if he was buying her things to make up for the decision he'd made. She seemed happy enough, and told him there were plenty of clubs and activities for her to participate in, but he couldn't help feeling she was putting on a brave face.

Yes, he'd noticed her playing Scrabble and indulging in a spot of crocheting, but at seventy-five, she wasn't old, just terribly infirm. Ever since she'd broken her hip at seventy, she hadn't been quite the same, and even installing a community alarm so she always had immediate help on hand hadn't given him much peace of mind. But his mother was nothing if not fiercely independent and it had taken a considerable number of further falls – more than he could count – before the decision had to be made to move her into Bay Park.

Of course, there was the advantage that the location couldn't be more beautiful, perched on the banks of Loch Lomond, but to Fraser's eye, his mother had aged ten years in less than three months.

He visited Saturday and Sunday and two to three nights a week, but still the guilt plagued him. And she was so proud of him – 'my wonderful son, the headteacher. Isn't he clever?' She was never done extolling his virtues; it was sweet if more than a little embarrassing. He hadn't the heart to tell her his placement at Heatherwood was just that – a placement. He was maternity cover, and when the head came back from mat leave, he'd be shunted somewhere else. He hadn't been able to bring himself to tell her he hadn't got the job as head at Ferntree.

As he locked the car, he felt a weight lift from his

shoulders momentarily. He'd make time for a quick drink whilst he was at Sugar and Spice. It was important to appreciate the little things in life – they were few and far between sometimes. The impending meeting with the education authority flitted through his mind before he brushed it aside. Fifteen minutes of peace, hopefully, before he had to head back. When he opened the door to the café, he was struck by how empty it was; last time he'd passed by, it had been crammed with shoppers and young mums and friends having meet-ups.

'Hi, Jacob, how are you?'

'Oh, hi, Mr McCafferty. How are things? Nice to see you in here.'

'Call me Fraser, please. Good, thanks. What's going on today?' He indicated the vacant seats.

'Oh, you've missed the rush. We had to turn people away today, and others took one look in the window, saw it was full and about-turned. Quite a few did come in and ask for drinks and cakes to go, too, though. There were fifteen yoga mums in here a minute ago. They've just left, hence all the empty seats.'

'Ah, I see. Well, that works even better for me, as I don't have much time. I have a meeting in half an hour.'

'Oh? You don't look too pleased about that,' Jacob said.

Fraser blew out a breath. 'Education authority. It usually goes one of two ways – they'll be dry or they'll be hard work. Sometimes both. One thing's for sure, it's never fun.'

'Hmm. What can I get you to make that a little bit easier for you?'

Fraser studied the drinks menu. 'A luxury hot

chocolate, please. I'm guessing that'll fill me up. They're usually topped with so much cream and marshmallows it's like a dessert. It's my guilty pleasure, but please, not a word to any of the kids. I'll never live it down.'

Jacob chuckled. 'One does try, and your secret's safe with me. Anything else?'

'Yeah, I'm in to get some cakes for my mum. She hasn't stopped raving about the ones I bought at the fair.'

'Oh, that's good to hear. Isn't it, Tabs?'

Fraser turned as the woman he'd spoken to at the fair's jewellery stall walked into the café from the area marked Private. He smiled. 'Hi.'

'Hi, Mr McCafferty.'

'Fraser, please.'

'Fraser. I hadn't realised who you were at the fair. Nice to meet you properly.' She held out her hand, and he enfolded it in his, noting the softness of her skin and her firm grip. When she retracted her hand, he felt a twinge of disappointment.

'You too.' Why did he feel so tongue-tied? It was like he was fifteen all over again.

'So, what can we tempt you with today? Perhaps one of our festive concoctions. Peppermint mocha, mulled pomegranate juice, cardamom rose milk; orange and clove-infused tea.'

He cleared his throat as he tried not to look at the curve of her neck or those gorgeous brown eyes. There was intelligence in her gaze, too, as she studied him.

She wasn't much shorter than him, which he also liked.

'Thanks, but Jacob already took my order.' He paused. 'So, you work here, too?'

Tabitha laughed. 'Only when it's really busy. I help

out. I'm a sleeping partner mainly.'

Fraser cleared his throat again. Was it hot in here, or did everything she say have a double meaning? Plus, she was with Jacob. Surely she wasn't flirting with him. 'Oh?' he managed finally.

'Jacob and I co-own it, although I mainly concentrate on my jewellery business now. I did the corporate life for a long time, and then realised when Lara came along that wasn't what I wanted any more.'

Lara. That was it. An unusual name. Lovely name. He recalled the sweet little girl at the fair the other day, and more recently Mrs Dalwood and Mrs Hopkins had told him they'd chosen Lara as their soloist for A Carol for Christmas. He hadn't heard her sing yet, but what did he know about singing? He just knew what he liked to listen to. Since the two teachers had been in charge of the choir and much of the nativity, with regards to the musical side of things, he wasn't going to intervene. They obviously knew what they were doing.

'That's quite a lot of work. You're clearly good at multitasking,' Fraser said.

Tabitha laughed. 'Something like that. I really like being part of the community here. You can probably guess from the accent that neither of us is originally from here. Are we, Jacob?'

'No. Down south originally. We've been here about a decade now.'

Tabitha smiled at him. 'Yes, once we arrived, we couldn't leave. Sorry, excuse me a second.' She dived forward to open the door for a mum who was trying to push a double pram through the doors. The woman looked familiar. Maybe another parent.

'Tabitha, how lovely to catch you here. You got time for a quick drink together?'

'Hot chocolate do you?' Tabitha asked, moving behind the counter and looking totally at ease. If she hadn't already told him, Fraser would have been able to tell she was one of the café owners simply from the confidence she exuded and her manner with the customers, although this one did seem to be more than a customer. A friend, perhaps. He found himself idly thinking that he wouldn't mind being Tabitha's friend. Where had that come from? He didn't have time for 'friendships'; he didn't even have time for platonic friendships.

Fraser turned to Jacob, then checked his watch. 'I'd better take my drink to go. Hmm, what cakes to choose? You have quite the selection here.'

That was putting it mildly. Fraser's traitorous stomach reminded him he hadn't eaten lunch yet. Maybe he could nab a cake for himself too.

'Did you want those you had at the fair, or do you think your mum would like to try something new?'

'Decisions, decisions,' Fraser said, tapping his fingers against the counter. 'Right, can you recommend me something, please?'

'With pleasure. This week's specials are mini spiced apple cider cakes; vanilla bean cupcakes with peppermint buttercream frosting; cranberry orange mini loaves and we have chiffon cake – a Chinese recipe that uses pandan, so the flavours are a mix of coconut and vanilla.'

Fraser screwed up his face, trying to imagine what that last one would taste like, and Jacob laughed.

'It's good. I promise you.'

'OK, I trust you.' Fraser smiled. 'In that case, can you

give me one of each of those, plus a chiffon cake separately, and can you give me a box of ten mixed cakes too?'

'Ah, is that you treating the office staff?' Jacob asked. 'I sometimes leave Paul some samples when I come to pick up Lara.'

That wasn't his plan, but he didn't want to get bogged down in the whole 'my mother's in a care home' story, so he simply let Jacob continue. He'd never seen any samples in the office. He supposed he probably didn't deserve them; it wasn't as if he'd been in the right frame of mind to fit in much with his team – not when he had all these clouds hanging over his head.

He glanced at his watch again. The next 'cloud' was due in his office in twenty minutes. Fortunately, he'd organised everything before he left, but even so, he was getting a little flustered. It was hard to play the jolly type, keen to have fun with everyone, when he knew what was hanging over them. The council were looking to make cuts and he didn't want to be responsible for anyone losing their job or not having their contract renewed. Deep down, he knew it wasn't his fault, but that didn't matter. He intended to leave Heatherwood with the staff roll at the same level or higher than when he took up his post.

Feeling like he had the world on his shoulders, Fraser hefted the boxes and the drink Jacob gave him and smiled to Tabitha as he passed.

'Bye, Fraser. See you soon,' Tabitha called, giving him a little wave.

He really hoped so, because right now with everything getting on top of him, despite his internal protests to the contrary, he could really do with a friend like Tabitha.

Three hours later, Fraser was caught in nose-to-tail rush-hour traffic, desiring nothing more than to put his head on the steering wheel and let the horn blast at full pelt. What had even been the purpose of that meeting with the board? They'd been holed up in his office for almost two hours then wandered around the school, sniffing at this and that. The school was as immaculate as it could be when it was full of several hundred primary school children. And the soul of the school shone from every pore. They hadn't commented on the incredible artwork on the walls, or any of the Christmas story stones the children had meticulously hand-painted, and which were on display in the main foyer. Nor had they shown any interest in the environmental Christmas corner, where Mrs Ralston, one of the primary four teachers, had worked with her class as part of their class topic on the environment, making snowmen out of plastic bottles they had painted white and embellished with felt and other materials from the craft boxes to create hats, scarves, carrot noses and googly eyes.

No, this trio from the board must have been Christmas-haters, because there wasn't one single reference to the upcoming festivities, despite the numerous exhibits around the school. Was it him? Had he done something wrong? He didn't think so – he'd prepared well for the meeting. He'd given the staff the heads-up they were coming in, and read through the minutes of the last four board meetings, but nothing had even raised a smile or an acknowledgement he and his staff were doing anything right, which he thought pretty harsh, given the school was already doing everything on a shoestring budget. He had seen that the previous head had requested funding for two additional members for the support team, but that had been vetoed.

The board had been closed books. He wasn't sure what he had expected, but being met by a wall of silence wasn't it. Once again, he mulled over why they'd scheduled a visit during one of the school's busiest times – Christmas. If they didn't want to see what the school did with the kids around Christmas time, then why bother to come? It didn't make sense, and it made him uneasy.

Finally, he arrived at Bay Park. He was looking forward to seeing his mum, although he knew it wasn't how many men of his age would want to spend their Friday night, and truth be told, were things different, neither would he. He'd have been happy wining and dining some fabulous woman. Fleetingly, an image of Tabitha with her long chestnut hair cascading over her shoulders popped into his mind. But this was his reality.

Hefting out the cakes and a few other bits and pieces he'd brought for his mum, he headed in to see how she was doing, hoping the chesty cough he'd noted she'd developed, when he'd been in a few days earlier, had improved. He hadn't liked the sound of that at all, and with constantly being stuck in a place with lots of other people, it was a breeding ground for bugs, just as much as a school was. Distractedly, he hoped he hadn't brought the bug in from school.

'Hi, Fraser. How are you doing?' Nancy, one of the receptionists, sat up a little straighter as he entered the building.

'Hi, Nancy. Nice jumper.' It was a little over the top, to the extent Fraser didn't know where to focus on first: the candy canes; Christmas trees – complete with actual miniature baubles and bells; Santa Claus in the middle; or the reindeer on each shoulder.

She grinned. 'Thanks. It has been a talking point all day.'

'I can imagine it has been quite the icebreaker.' He paused then said, 'Have you seen Mum today?'

'Yes, she came out for a chat earlier. I think she thought you were coming this afternoon.'

Fraser frowned. 'But she knows I'm working in the afternoon Monday to Friday.'

'That's what she said. Maybe she got mixed up with the days. It happens in here sometimes.'

That was partly what he'd been afraid of when she'd entered the care home. But did he have anything else to worry about? She wasn't beginning to forget things, too, was she? He'd need to keep an eye on her. One more thing to worry about.

Realising that Nancy was eyeing him expectantly, he said, 'Sorry, I was daydreaming there. Here, these are for you and the rest of the staff.' He handed her the box of cakes.

'Oh, thank you. That's so kind. Sugar and Spice? Wow, this is the place your mum has been banging on about ever since you brought those cakes in from the Christmas fair.'

'That's the one. And you're welcome.' He explained to her as best he could what all the cakes were, and in part their origin, as she was genuinely interested, then left her with a smile on her face as he sought out his mum.

He found her in one of the activity rooms, with another six residents. An array of craft materials lay in front of them. They'd evidently been having a workshop of some kind.

'Hi, Mum.' He bent and kissed her cheek as her face lit

up on seeing him.

'Aw, Fraser, I'm so glad you're here. I thought you'd have been here hours ago.'

Fraser's disquiet ratcheted up a notch. 'No, Mum. Remember, I need to work until around four, even on a Friday, then there's traffic.'

'But it's so dark outside.'

'It's because we're almost at the shortest day. So, tell me, what have you all been making here?'

His mum picked up her offering and turned it this way and that. 'A Christmas wreath. Do you like it?'

He had to admit, she'd done a good job. It wasn't quite finished, but the mix of red berries, pine cones, a few tasteful red ribbons, slices of dried orange and cinnamon sticks did look very festive.

'Will you help me finish it? I made it for you,' she said, her gnarled hand grasping his.

'For me?' Fraser's brow creased.

'Well, yes. I mean, I don't have a front door any more, not an external one at least, so what would be the point of making it for myself? Far better for you to take it and enjoy it, don't you think?'

Fraser's throat tightened as he fought to keep a handle on his emotions. Her throwaway comment had unconsciously hit home. Inwardly, he took a deep breath and then rallied. 'Of course. It will look great on my front door.'

'Excellent. I know what you're like. I bet you've been too busy to put up a tree. At least this way, you'll have something festive to mark the season.'

His throat constricted further and he knew tears weren't far away.

'Thanks. Before I forget, I have a little something for you.' Conscious of the fact he didn't have enough for everyone, he said, 'If you give me your key, I'll put it in your room and you can check it out once you've finished here.'

'Ooh, I like surprises. Thank you.' She passed him the key.

He rushed off, calling over his shoulder, 'I'll be back in a minute.'

When he reached her room, he sat the box of festive cakes on the bedside table and then let the tears flow.

Chapter Nine

'I wrote my letter to Santa the other day,' Ivy said to Lara as she tapped her pencil against her lips. Lara noticed she often did that when she was concentrating. They were working in pairs doing fractions and remainders using the Christmas-themed resources Mrs Hopkins had given them. Lara loved maths, but Ivy wasn't so keen. She was better at spelling.

'I haven't written mine yet.'

Ivy's eyes were wide. 'Really? Well, you'd better hurry up or you'll miss the last Christmas post.'

Lara frowned. 'Is that a thing?'

Ivy nodded. 'Yeah. The lady in the post office was telling my mum the other day that the last post to America had already passed. And the North Pole is further away than America.'

Lara frowned again. Was it? Wasn't the North Pole somewhere between Denmark and Greenland? America was further away than that, she knew, as she'd studied the map in her mum's office. She'd check again when she got home, and make sure she wrote her letter to Santa. Perhaps she could even start at playtime and finish it off at home. She didn't want very much, so it wouldn't take long.

'What do you want for Christmas anyway?' Ivy asked as

she scribbled an answer in the box. Lara glanced over, then looked at her own answer and back at Ivy's. She added up the numbers in her head again, then put her finger on Ivy's page. 'Sorry, that answer's wrong. And for Christmas, I'd like a new scooter and a couple of games.'

'Aargh! Is it?' Ivy frowned for a second then rubbed out her answer and input another. Lara craned her neck. Yep, this time it was the right answer.

'What games are you asking for?'

'Horrible Histories and Around the World,' Lara said, glancing up as she chose another challenge card from the maths set.

'I love Horrible Histories, the books and the TV show.'

'Me too. That's why I want the board game.'

'There's a lot of talking going on over here, girls, and it doesn't all seem maths-related. Are we finished yet?' Mrs Hopkins said.

Lara looked up. 'I've just finished.'

'Excellent. It's almost time for choir practice, and we need about fifteen minutes beforehand to work on your solo. Mrs Rogers will be in shortly to take over the class, whilst myself and Mrs Dalwood take those for choir. Have you been practising a little at home?'

Lara nodded. 'I have, but Mum eventually said I had to rest my vocal chords in case I strained them.'

Mrs Hopkins smiled. 'Very wise. Right, five minutes and we'll go.' She turned away and said, 'Five minutes, everyone, to finish off your Christmas maths. If you don't finish it, feel free to take it home and finish it there, or if you have any problems, see me after lunch. Those who are going to choir, Mrs Rogers will send you down in about twenty minutes.'

'Right, Lara, how are you feeling?' asked Bella, thinking the poor child looked terrified.

'Good.' Lara fiddled with the edge of her cardigan.

'No need to be nervous. You're going to be just fine. Do you need some water? You have some high notes to reach.'

'Yes, please,' Lara said, clearing her throat.

Bella handed her a paper cup of water and Lara drank from it thirstily. When Lara had finished her drink, Bella said, 'OK, let's get started.' She pressed the play button on the iPod for the music and the melodious notes of 'Joy to the World' filled the room.

'Now, Lara, start gently at first. If you can't reach the high notes, don't worry. This is simply to warm your voice up. Do you remember the words?'

Lara shook her head.

'Do you remember the tune?'

'Yes, miss.'

'OK, then here's a sheet with the words on. You can sing this and then we'll try "O Holy Night". Sound good?'

Lara nodded again.

Poor thing. She still looks terrified. 'Lara, you'll be fine, but remember, if you don't want to do this, you don't have to. Just because you have an amazing voice, you don't have to sing in front of everyone if you don't want to. Got it?'

'But won't I be letting everyone down if I don't sing?'

Bella smiled at her and patted her shoulder. 'Lara, no, you wouldn't be letting anyone down. We'd be letting *you* down if we asked you to do this and you weren't comfortable with it. So, if, and only if, you want to sing, give me a nod when you're ready. OK?' She moved the song back to the start again and waited for Lara's signal.

After about twenty seconds, Lara took a deep breath, closed her eyes then nodded before opening her eyes again and looking at the sheet.

Bella pressed play and watched as Lara, like they'd discussed, started off gently, then built up until she was hitting the high notes of 'Joy to the World'.

Bella stared, marvelling at this child and her incredible voice. She was kicking herself for not having noticed it before. Lara had kept it well hidden, but now it had been unleashed, Bella was totally enthralled. She bet when the parents came to listen to the annual choir competition in Winstanton's market square, there wouldn't be anyone who wasn't moved to tears.

When Lara finished singing, Bella beamed at her and clapped loudly. 'Lara, that was fantastic. Well done.'

Lara reddened and even the tips of her ears turned pink.

'I really like that carol,' Lara said. 'It's one of my mum's favourites. I just didn't know all the words off by heart.'

Bella looked at her. She was such a dear little thing, easy-going. A pretty girl, with long chestnut, wavy hair, which fell way past her shoulders, and she had such delicate features. Wistfully, Bella thought if she ever had a child, she'd like it to be like Lara. She could tell she really wanted to do well, to please, but she also hoped she had enough confidence to stand up for herself too. People who were too kind sometimes got taken advantage of, and she should know.

'Well, you did a great job.' She paused then said, 'Would you like to sing "O Holy Night" now?'

'Yes, please.'

Bella found the music and pressed play on the iPod.

As she listened to Lara sing, once again, tears threatened. She wondered if she was the only one who'd feel this way or if Amy or Paul would too. She'd noted the janitor's presence when she was talking to Lara about the solo the other day.

When Lara stopped this time, Bella was about to congratulate her, when clapping sounded from the doorway. Bella spun round to see the headmaster standing watching them with a huge smile on his face.

'Mrs Hopkins, Lara, that was sensational. I heard it from my office and had to come and witness it properly.'

Lara smiled at him, then he said, 'Lara, I hope you realise not many people can sing like that. You have an exceptional gift, and I look forward to hearing more from you.'

When she blushed, he said, 'I mean, what better excuse do I have to leave all that boring paperwork on my desk than coming to listen to such beautiful singing? Well done.'

He turned to Bella. 'And good choice, Mrs Hopkins.'

Bella felt herself flushing now. She wondered out of her and Lara, who was reddest. Praise, from Mr McCafferty? He hadn't exactly been warm with the staff, and came across as rather standoffish, but here he was congratulating her on a job well done. Wonders would never cease. Perhaps she was being unfair. He did seem rather stressed a lot of the time, his lips pressed in a thin line. She'd barely seen him smile, and she knew he'd given Paul an especially hard time, most recently over the layout of the hall for a parents' evening, when he'd given specific instructions. Poor Paul was finding it difficult adapting to having a new boss. Mr McCafferty's arrival had upset the applecart all right.

The stampeding sound of many feet heralded the arrival of the rest of the choir and Amy and Mr McCafferty stood aside to let the pupils file in. She was slightly alarmed when he showed no signs of leaving; instead, he leant against the wall and folded his arms as if settling in for some time.

Flustered under the watchful eye of the headmaster, Bella dropped some song sheets she'd printed off for the choir, and Lara bent to help her pick them up.

'It's OK to be nervous, miss,' Lara whispered, and Bella gave her a measured look then leant in and said conspiratorially, 'See, nerves get the better of all of us sometimes.'

They smiled at each other and stood up, then Bella gave Lara half of the song sheets to distribute to the choir whilst she handed out the rest. As Bella passed Amy, her friend raised an eyebrow at her. 'Flavour of the month?' she murmured.

'Hardly,' Bella muttered back, 'but he was highly impressed with Lara.'

'Hard not to be. She has the makings of a star. If we don't win that competition with her voice, the council have rigged it.'

Bella laughed, but noting the head glancing at his watch, she gave instructions to the choir, Amy pressed play on the first song and choir practice was soon underway.

When practice had finished and the bell had rung for lunch, Bella thanked the children and told them when the next rehearsal would be. She and Amy had nine days to make this work before the grand performance in the town's square, and she wanted to ensure all the children had fun, and that Lara, in particular, shone, because her life had been brighter since Lara began singing. OK, it was still awful – she was still getting divorced, and she would still be alone this Christmas – but Lara had provided a tiny ray of hope and sunshine in the darkness, and for that she would be forever grateful.

Paul sank into his recliner, pulled the TV magazine towards him and flipped on the television to watch the news. It had been a long day and he'd just gritted all the pavements on the approach to the school, and as much of the playground as he could feasibly cover. His fingers were still numb from the cold. The weather forecast was due on in five minutes and he wanted an update on that too. It was currently -2 °C if the app on his phone was to be relied upon. It had certainly felt like it, and he'd wished he hadn't left his gloves in the house that morning. He really needed to keep a spare pair at work. His knuckles were red raw and he'd have put them next to the roaring fire Elaine had lit, were it not for the fact he knew it would be painful. No, far better to let his body acclimatise and return to room temperature on its own.

'Cup of tea?' Elaine popped her head around the living room door. 'I'm making one for me and Susan. Christine's due shortly.'

'I'd love one, thanks.'

Elaine bent and kissed his head. Her lips were warm, unlike his head, which was about as warm as a bag of ice straight from the freezer.

When she left the room, he settled back and closed his eyes momentarily. Elaine's sisters could drink tea for Britain. That was all they seemed to do – well, that and chat. He let the newscaster's droning on wash over him. Days like today he could do without. He was getting too old for hefting sacks of grit around. And although he'd tried to ignore it, in a vain attempt to fool himself he wasn't as old as his sixty-four years, he definitely had arthritis and it was never more obvious than it had been today. He felt as if people miles away could have heard the creaking of his bones when he bent down.

He was looking forward to a quiet night in with a film and either a takeaway or whatever Elaine had cooked. Since she was only part-time these days, in her job at the library, she tended to do the majority of the cooking during the week and he cooked at the weekend. He made a mean chilli, even if he did say so himself. That's what he really fancied, but he didn't think there was any left in the freezer. He'd batch cook some next weekend.

Elaine had been busy this week, with her sisters visiting from England. They were going back tomorrow, and although he liked them well enough, two weekends of a man's life with his sisters-in-law in tow was two weekends too many.

So much for his quiet night in. Cackling and giggling emanated from the kitchen, then the door opened again and Elaine thrust a cup of tea at him, almost as if it were a weapon. 'There you go.'

'Thanks.'

She turned and headed back to the kitchen. On the one hand, he felt slighted that they didn't come to join him in the living room. It was borderline rude, after all. On the other hand, he was grateful to be left in peace. But what could they possibly have to talk about after ten days together? Elaine only worked three days a week, three hours a day, so she'd seen her sisters every single day.

He picked up his Lee Child book and muted the TV, then took a sip of his tea. As he placed his tea down on the side table, he noticed some cruise brochures. So, Jacob had been right. He'd wondered when she was going to wheel those out. He'd thought it would have been far sooner, but he supposed with his sisters-in-law here, Elaine hadn't had the chance.

He leafed through one of them: Caribbean cruises – Puerto Rico, Saint Lucia, Saint Kitts and Nevis. Yes, those all sounded great … and faraway, but how would they ever afford something like that? He was busy working out if he could afford a takeaway. With the increase in the price of their electricity bill, they'd had to make a number of sacrifices.

I suppose at least I won't have to use my oven or microwave if I get a takeaway.

He gave a bitter laugh. It wasn't funny. Their bill had more than doubled and it didn't look like it would change anytime soon, and here was Elaine planning Caribbean cruises. Her timing was lousy.

His eyes fell on several more magazines over on the coffee table. Great. Elaine was obviously going on an all-out offensive. He sighed. He didn't have the headspace for this right now and he just wanted to thaw out, watch TV, eat and sleep. The following day's weather was meant to be bad, although how bad he wouldn't know until morning. For now, he could only do himself the favour of remembering his lined fleecy gloves.

'That's Susan gone,' Elaine said, tapping him on the arm.

He must have fallen asleep. Paul roused himself, feeling groggy but fortunately considerably warmer than when he'd arrived home.

'I thought Christine was coming,' he said, rubbing his eyes in an attempt to return to full wakefulness.

'No, the weather's closing in. That's why Susan got a cab back to the hotel. At least it's not far.'

'Is it snowing?' Paul asked, jerking upwards.

Elaine shook her head. 'No, but it will do later. I heard on the radio that it's expected around eleven tonight.'

Paul yawned. 'What time is it?'

Elaine smiled and said, 'Time for dinner. I made steak pie earlier. It's that kind of night.'

Paul sighed with relief. His stomach was reminding him he hadn't eaten yet and Elaine's steak pie was to die for, although she deviated from the mainstream recipe and added link sausages, which he preferred.

December was made for hearty food like this. He loved being indoors watching snow falling, but equally he loved returning from the cold to a warming bowl of homemade soup or hearty fare such as steak pie, chicken pie, cottage pie – actually, now he was seeing a recurring theme – pie. It did tend to hit the spot though.

'Do you want a hand?'

Elaine shook her head. 'No, you relax. It won't be long. Maybe you could have a look through those magazines I left on the table.'

He caught her eye as she was leaving the room and she winked. His wife was too clever by half.

'Elaine, you've outdone yourself. That was exceptionally

good tonight.' Paul set his cutlery in the middle of the plate as he always did, signalling he was finished.

'Thanks. It was good, wasn't it? Anyway, any room for dessert?'

Paul shook his head. 'Not now. Maybe later. I'm stuffed.'

'So,' Elaine said as she cleared the table, 'what did you think of the cruises?'

Paul nodded. 'Well, they look very nice, obviously. Did you have a particular one in mind?'

'Now you come to mention it, there's a fourteen-night one at the beginning of March, leaving from Fort Lauderdale. It's a really good deal.'

Paul couldn't help thinking Elaine's idea of a really good deal and his were probably two different things.

'March? But that's during term-time.'

'Yes, but your birthday is on Valentine's Day, so you'll be retired by then.'

Paul raised his eyes to the ceiling as if imploring it to give him strength, then he looked directly at his wife and said, 'Elaine, I can't keep telling you this and you not hearing it. I am not retiring at sixty-five. I have asked to stay on for another couple of years. I love my job.'

'Paul, nobody loves their job so much they choose not to retire. Name one other person who has done what you're suggesting. People are queuing up to retire earlier, but we're all being made to work more and more these days. Why would you want to continue?'

How could he tell her that the school gave him purpose, that if he had to get up every day and listen to her inane chatter about shopping and book club and Netflix shows, he'd slowly lose his mind? She was happy to spend time with him, sure, and he her, but he didn't think he'd be the sort of person who'd cope well with too much free time on his hands.

'Elaine, that's what I want to do, and that's what I've told the school, and what they've told the council,' he said firmly.

'And what about what I want, Paul? Have you ever thought about that?'

She crashed the plates down on the table and stormed out of the room, slamming the door so hard it bounced on its hinges.

Paul sighed. Not the quiet night in he'd planned at all.

Chapter Ten

'Mrs Hopkins, can I go see Mr Fairbairn, please? I think I left my trainers in the changing room yesterday.'

'Of course, Lara, but be quick. You all have only half an hour left to write the rest of your Christmas letters to the children at St John's.'

Lara's friend Abigail went to St John's. Every year each of the new primary sixes exchanged a Christmas letter with the neighbouring school. They told them what they wanted for Christmas, how they would spend the holidays, and what Christmas films and activities they were most looking forward to. Of course, they could do all this already, by messaging or emailing, but the whole point was for everyone to receive a nice letter at Christmas time and remember that in the past, the technology they had now hadn't existed.

Lara smiled. It made her laugh that her mum still sent Christmas cards to relatives and friends far away, in Asia, America and Australia. From what her mum had told her of her life when she was her age, she had travelled a lot. And when she wasn't travelling, she and her uncle Jacob had gone to boarding school. Lara couldn't imagine going to boarding school. She'd miss everyone so much – no Ivy, no Mum, no Uncle Jacob or Aunt Sophie. The idea gave her the shivers.

When she reached the janitor's office, there was no one there. She searched the usual places nearby, but there was no sign of him. She was about to ask the office if they had her trainers or knew where Mr Fairbairn was, when he trudged in the front door of the school, wiping his boots on the mat and sighing.

'Cold out there, is it, Paul?' one of the ladies in the office asked. Lara couldn't make out whose voice it was and the wall was in the way, so she couldn't see.

'Absolutely bitter. I'm surprised it hasn't snowed yet, especially given the forecast.'

'Yes, weather forecasters never get it wrong.' The woman chuckled and Mr Fairbairn smiled.

As he headed towards his office, he stopped upon seeing Lara. 'Lara, are you looking for me?'

'Yes. I left my trainers in the changing room yesterday. They're black with pink and they have my name inside.'

'Indeed they do,' said Mr Fairbairn. 'And yes, I have them. And well done to your mum for putting name tags in them. Half the children in this school, their clothes have no tags on them, then they and their parents wonder why stuff goes missing.'

Not sure how to respond to that, Lara stayed silent, but as she followed him into his office, she said, 'I like your Christmas tree. Can I press the button?'

Mr Fairbairn smiled. 'Sure. Just turn the dial down underneath, otherwise the music will blast out and we'll both get in trouble.' He whispered the last part and Lara grinned before following his instructions and watching the tree lights spring to life one by one, then the tree danced as the sound of 'Deck the Halls' came out of it, although it was rather quiet, given she'd turned the sound down.

'Are you feeling Christmassy, Mr Fairbairn?' Lara asked.

Mr Fairbairn hesitated as if he'd been about to say something but changed his mind, then finally said, 'I feel the most Christmassy when I'm here in this school, watching all of you perform in the nativity, hearing you sing both in the choir and as a soloist, and as I walk down these corridors, looking at all the fabulous crafts and artwork you and all the other children have created.'

Lara nodded then screwed up her face and gazed at him. 'Have you made anything this year?'

Mr Fairbairn laughed. 'No, I'm too old for that sort of thing.'

Lara shook her head. 'My mum and my uncle Jacob say adults are never too old and that you're only as old as you feel.'

Mr Fairbairn said, 'Well, I must be about a hundred and two, as that's how old I feel right now.'

Lara tilted her head. 'Are you ill, or have you hurt yourself?'

'No, nothing like that. I have a lot on my mind. I could retire in a few months, you know.' Mr Fairbairn seemed to have gone off into a daydream.

'Really? Are you that old?' Lara said, then covered her hand with her mouth. 'Sorry. I shouldn't have said that. It's just, you don't look that old.'

Mr Fairbairn smiled then said, 'Thanks for the compliment, but yes, I'm old enough to retire.'

'What would you do if you retired?' Lara said.

Mr Fairbairn paused. 'Do you know something, Lara? I don't actually know.'

'Do you have any hobbies?'

Mr Fairbairn took some time to think, then he said, 'Not really. Well, I mean, I like cooking, but I already do that at the weekend.'

Lara thought for a moment. 'You could do a course, then maybe you'd be like one of those TV chefs and get your own show.'

Mr Fairbairn laughed. 'I don't think that's likely. Maybe I could learn to bake. I do like cakes, although I've never been much of a baker.'

'Uncle Jacob is a great baker. Maybe he could show you. If you come to the craft night later, you could ask him.'

'Thanks, Lara, that's very kind, but I don't think your uncle Jacob would have time to teach an old man like me how to bake cupcakes.'

'Oh, it wouldn't only be cupcakes. It would be all sorts.' She rhymed off about twenty cakes, then seeing the smile on Mr Fairbairn's face, she stopped. 'What is it?'

'Nothing. Just thinking of another possibility.'

'Oh? What?'

'Too early to say, Lara. But thanks for the inspiration. Now you'd best run along to class, or I'll be getting in trouble.'

As she was leaving his office, Mr Fairbairn called after her, 'Don't forget your trainers.'

Lara swung back into the room and picked up her trainers. 'Thanks. And six o'clock for the craft evening, if you're interested.'

As Lara trotted back to class, she smiled. All was going according to plan.

The snow began to fall as Fraser was heading to his car. Typical. Forecasters were always out, whether by a few hours or a few days. Hopefully, it wouldn't come to much. He had to get over to Bay Park later, but first he had to nip into town for a few things. He also had an appointment with a solicitor, at his mum's insistence, in order to arrange power of attorney. Although he knew it made sense, it saddened him because it felt as if they were already accepting that at some point she would no longer be there, and whilst he knew this to be true, he really didn't need reminding of it.

As he drove towards town, the sight of all the Christmas lights in the windows lifted his mood, conjuring up cosy scenes of couples cuddling by the fireside; children begging their parents to put up the Christmas tree as early as possible; dads replacing bulb after bulb on the tree lights, trying to work out which one was faulty and finally giving up and driving to the hardware store to buy new ones. He missed those days as he'd had a rather idyllic childhood, although he did wish he'd had siblings to share it with. He hadn't been a greedy child, so he'd never really wanted all that many presents, and would have far preferred a brother or sister to play with. And once his dad died, it was only him and his mum. That was probably why they were as close as they were, although they had been close even back then; the three of them had been.

He'd love to be a part of what was going on behind one of those windows, to feel like he belonged again. He hadn't even bothered putting up a tree. What was the point? His mum thought he was too busy, but the truth was it would seem so sad, sitting there all on its own, with only him to see it.

Without his mum to enjoy it with him, or come visit, it was just an exercise in futility.

Anyway, he'd had enough of a pity party. Time to shake a leg and get on with it. He was looking forward to seeing her later, but first he needed to meet with the solicitor.

Thank goodness that was over with. First a school board meeting then seeing a solicitor. The latter was right up there on his list of all-time favourite things to do, directly above watching paint dry.

Now he deserved a treat, and since he'd intended to drop into T&J's to buy his mum a few new novels to read, he decided to buy something for himself too. Something that wasn't non-fiction for a change, nor a Booker Prize winner and thus considered worthy. Maybe something like a thriller or a crime novel.

As he was about to cross the street to T&J's, he looked longingly towards Sugar and Spice with its welcoming glow and inviting ambiance. He shivered, only then noticing how much more snow had fallen whilst he'd been in the solicitor's. The orange flashing light of a gritting lorry passed him and he stood back from the kerb to avoid being sprayed with grit and rock salt.

He crossed the road as the door to Sugar and Spice opened and a couple spilled out onto the pavement, laughing and wrapping their scarves around themselves.

Inside the bookshop, he wandered around, revelling in its nooks and crannies. It was such a find of a place, and it had a fabulous kids' section too – as a child, he'd have enjoyed being able to lose himself in a book in here.

He loved the fact there were comfy armchairs to sit in, so you could browse and sit and read a few pages, or chapters, of the books you were interested in.

After wandering around the different sections of the rabbit warren store for about fifteen minutes, he plunked himself down in a chair and began to read the blurbs of the stack of books he'd chosen.

As he read, he realised how thirsty he was, and how great it would have been if he could have had a cup of tea, or something stronger, to go with his reading.

'Hello, stranger,' a voice said behind him.

Fraser looked up into Tabitha's face, which was absent of makeup, and which made her look like a fresh-faced teenager, instead of the thirty-something, probably late-thirty-something he imagined her to be.

He put down his book. 'Hi. Fancy seeing you here.'

'Well, I do own the shop next door.'

'That's true. Do you want to join me?' He gestured to the navy and cream corduroy armchair opposite, which matched his.

'Sure.' She sank into the armchair. 'What are you reading?'

He picked the book back up. 'This one's Grisham. One of my favourite authors.' Then he turned to the stack on the side table between them. 'Here we have Michael Connelly, Tess Gerritsen, Harlan Coben, Lisa Scottoline and Karin Slaughter.'

'Ah, so you're a big crime and thriller fan then?'

Fraser pursed his lips. 'You could say that. What about you?'

'What kind of books do you think I'm into?' Tabitha said, a smile playing on her lips.

'Oh, reading's such a personal thing. I don't think I could guess.'

Tabitha smiled. 'Well, let me narrow it down for you. Do I seem like someone who would like high fantasy involving dragons, goblins and shapeshifters, or someone who would be more at home reading romantic fiction and watching romantic comedies on Netflix?'

Fraser's heart sank. Was this a test? If so, he had the most awful feeling he was about to fail it. She *was* late thirties, he reckoned, now he could see her at closer range, without it appearing odd that he was looking at her. He knew fantasy had had a huge resurgence of late, but was it feasible that this woman, and mum, was a high fantasy fan?

'Hmm, that's a toughie. Do I get any clues?' He was careful not to flirt with her. She was, after all, married to Jacob, who was a great guy, but she was naturally beautiful, in an understated way, and she gave off the vibe of someone who didn't take herself too seriously and knew how to have fun, and he found that very attractive. How unfortunate that he was drawn to Tabitha, when she was unavailable.

'Clues, you say? OK, you can ask me three questions. How about that?'

He nodded. 'Fine. I can work with that.' He thought for a second then said, 'Question one. Have you ever played Dungeons and Dragons?'

'Yes. Jacob is really into it.'

Fraser's heart sank again. She and Jacob really were inextricably linked, and then there was Lara to figure into the equation. Not that he'd ever consider going after another man's wife, plus Tabitha was a pupil's parent. Still, he could dream; it was all he could do. And he could totally see Jacob being into D&D. Personally, it had never held any appeal for him, but each to their own.

'OK. Question number two.' He debated what to ask then finally came up with, '*Love Actually* or *Lord of the Rings*?'

Tabitha grinned. 'No question. *Love Actually.*'

Fraser quirked an eyebrow. 'I did not see that coming. Hmm, final question.' He steepled his fingers together and said, 'World-building or character development?'

'Hands-down, character development. So, have you reached any conclusions?'

Fraser tapped his steepled fingers against his lips, as if deep in thought. 'Well, I estimate it has to be romance.'

Tabitha's lips curved up at the edges. 'Nope! Not even close. Actually, I'm a bit of a magpie, which means I like to read across various genres.' She patted the pile of books on the table. 'These are some of my favourite authors, and crime and thriller are my favourite genres.'

Fraser gaped. 'You mean, you put me through all that, and all along we had the same taste in books?'

Tabitha winked. 'It was fun, though, wasn't it?'

'I guess so. Anyway–' he stood up '–I need to choose something for my mum. She's not into crime and thriller.'

'What does she like?' Tabitha asked, also standing. His breath caught as she was so close to him he could smell her shampoo. She wasn't much shorter than him, so they were almost nose to nose, less than half an arm's width apart.

'Book-club fiction, and historical romance. It's not my thing, so I really don't know where to start.'

'Not my thing either, but they're really good here at giving recommendations. C'mon.' She began to walk away and then turned back. 'Are you buying any of those?' She pointed to the stack of books he'd picked up.

He was so flustered in her company, he couldn't even make a decision. He'd planned on buying two, but found himself saying, 'Yes, all of them.'

'Nice.' She smiled. 'And a great way to support a small business. Tom and Jerry are lovely and this is the best independent bookshop around. People come here from all over.'

'Tom and Jerry?'

'Yeah. The owners?' At his blank expression, she continued, 'T&J? Tom and Jerry.'

'I had no idea,' said Fraser. 'That's pretty funny.'

Tabitha laughed. 'They get teased all the time. Lots of cat and mouse jokes. They even have a book to keep a record of the ribbings they take.'

'No way!' Fraser said.

'I'm not kidding. My favourite is the guy who came in and asked for a book on catching mice, and they thought it was another mickey-take, but he honestly wanted a book on mice-catching.'

'Ha ha, that must have been embarrassing – for them – and confusing for the customer.'

'Yes, not least because he had no idea they were called Tom and Jerry … a bit like you.'

'I'll be careful not to make any jokes, although it's tempting now I know I'd go in the book.'

'Oh, Lara's in it loads of times.'

Fraser frowned. 'Really?' Lara struck him as a sweet, polite, rule-abiding little girl.

'Yeah. My daughter has a wicked sense of humour. She came in last week and asked for The Three *Mouseketeers*. Last month, she asked for *The Cat in the Hat*, and the other day she came in and asked for some Japanese author's book featuring cats. They're used to her by now. She also gets a lollipop from them if they like her offering enough.'

Fraser smiled. He liked this place even more now, and he wanted to meet Tom and Jerry.

'That's settled then. Let's go ask them for some recommendations,' Tabitha said with a smile.

Chapter Eleven

Paul had fully intended going home and having that quiet night he'd been coveting, but life had ways of making him change his plans when he least expected it. Earlier in the day he'd messaged Elaine to ask if she needed him to pick anything up for dinner on the way home and she'd replied saying her sisters' flight had been cancelled and she was having dinner out with them this evening – unspoken message – he wasn't invited. He'd thought of splurging on that takeaway he'd debated the other night, but on a whim, he'd gone into town.

Lara had got him thinking about his interests. He didn't have much time to indulge them these days. In the past he'd loved photography, mainly landscapes and wildlife.

If they did go on this cruise Elaine had her heart set on, at least if he had an up-to-date camera, he could dabble a bit more convincingly. Yes, smartphones had really good cameras these days, but he wasn't interested in the speed or editing the photos or sharing them. He wanted to be able to take high-quality photos in all lights and to be able to manually manage aperture, focus and exposure.

Hidden down a tiny side street near the church a superb little camera shop. He'd go there then maybe he'd pop into Sugar and Spice if they were still open and have an early dinner before the craft night started. Maybe he'd even stay for that. Who knew. Today was all about new beginnings, and it had all started with the kernel of a seed little Lara had sown earlier.

'Paul, hi. What can I get you?' Jacob asked as Paul came in, shaking the snow off his boots, then taking off his gloves and putting them in the pockets of his puffy jacket.

'Hi, Jacob. Any soup left?'

'You're in luck. We made extra earlier, as I knew we might have some takers at the craft night. Is that what you're here for?'

'I don't exactly know. Your Lara was selling it to me today, suggesting I come.'

Jacob smiled. 'Was she? Ha, we'll make an entrepreneur out of that girl yet. Anyway, we have butternut squash, tom yum and lentil.'

'Hmm. What's tom yum? Sounds Asian.'

'Good guess,' said Jacob. 'It's a spicy, aromatic Thai soup. Delicious, I promise.'

'Sold,' said Paul.

'Great. Grab a seat and I'll bring it over.'

Paul glanced around and saw to his dismay that the café was really busy. There wasn't a free table.

'You can sit here if you want, son,' a voice said.

'Hi, Stanley. I didn't see you there. That would be great,' said Paul, pulling out a chair.

'It's always busy at the craft nights. I've been coming for years.'

'I've never been before, not in all the years I've lived

here. I don't know whether to stay tonight or have my soup and head home.'

'Oh, you should absolutely stay, son. The Christmas craft session is the best one. I think I made half of my Christmas decorations here.'

Paul laughed. 'I haven't even got my tree up yet.'

'What? It'll be January before you know it. Is all that snow outside not incentive enough? Not getting you in the Christmas spirit?'

'Hmm. I don't know. I'm just not feeling as Christmassy as usual this year.'

Stanley frowned. 'How can you not be Christmassy when you're surrounded by all the kids and their activities at the school every day?'

Paul sighed. 'It's a long story, Stanley, but the main problem is, I'm of retiring age next year, and I'm afraid in case this is the last time I get to see it all – at the school, I mean.'

'Nonsense.' Stanley patted his arm. 'Even after you retire, that school will have you back as an honorary guest for as long as you want to go. Remember, that's what they did with Charlie, the lollipop man.'

'I know, but it won't be the same as being in the school, every day, being part of it all.'

Stanley tilted his head to one side. 'True. But it sounds to me like you're not ready to retire yet.'

Paul held Stanley's gaze for a minute. 'Stanley, you're right.'

Stanley nodded and gave Paul a knowing smile when Jacob brought over his soup.

'There you go. Anything else?'

'No, I'm good, thanks, Jacob. I'll probably get a drink

once I've had this.'

'No worries.' He turned to Stanley. 'Stanley, can I get you anything?'

'I'll have one of those cinnamon latte numbers, Jacob, thank you.'

Jacob, his hands on his hips, said, 'Latte? At this time? You won't sleep.'

'Maybe I want to finish that book I'm reading,' Stanley said.

'Stanley, you'll get me in trouble with the care home if I take you back and you're up half the night.'

Stanley rolled his eyes. 'Oh, OK then, give me a hot chocolate, and don't be stingy with the marshmallows.'

Jacob smiled. 'Coming right up.'

As he walked away, Stanley called after him, 'Or the whipped cream.'

Paul stared at Stanley. 'You two get on well.'

Stanley nodded. 'Yes, well, Jacob and Natalie were both really good to me after my Edie died. Eleven years ago now.'

'I'm sorry.'

'Oh, it's all right, but those two helped me put my life back together, learn what I needed to do to go on after Edie. Words will never describe how grateful I am to Jacob, and Natalie, when she was here. After that, I came in at least a few times a week, until I moved to Bay Park. Now, Jacob comes and picks me up and brings me down to these events so I don't miss out.'

'That's really kind of him.'

'Isn't it? He's such a good boy. Really looks after me.'

'And he bakes great cakes,' broke in Paul.

'Oh, tell me about it. I used to be thin!'

Paul laughed as he took in Stanley's rake-thin physique. 'OK, maybe I will stay for the craft session.'

'That's the spirit. You'll be glad you did. I promise.'

'Hey, Jacob. Where's Tabitha?' Valerie undid the buttons on her coat, which was covered in a fine smattering of snow. The snow had been off, on, off, on much of the day.

'Hi, Valerie. She went into Tom and Jerry's not long ago.' He threw a glance in Lara's direction once Ivy headed towards her and whispered, 'She was away to get some books for Lara's stocking.'

'Ah. Right, where to sit? Oh, give me a sec, Jacob.' Valerie smiled at the elderly couple who were vacating a table, tore off her coat and flung it over one of the chairs, then strode back to the counter.

'No twins?' Jacob said. 'I'm not about to discover you've left them outside in the snow by mistake?'

'Don't even get me started!' Valerie could feel her stress levels spiking.

Jacob's brow furrowed. 'Everything OK?'

'Not exactly.' She blew out a breath. 'Munro was supposed to be home to look after the twins so I could bring Ivy to the craft session, but he had a meeting that overran. I've had to leave them with a friend until he gets in.'

'Oh no. Not conducive to a relaxed experience, but hey, look on the bright side, you're here now, Ivy's about to be scooped up by Lara, and you can chill for a bit.'

She shot him a grateful smile. 'Thanks, Jacob. I really did need reminding of that. Pumpkin spice latte, please. Decaff.'

'Go and relax. I'll bring it over. Maybe you should text Tabitha and tell her you're here.'

'I will do.'

As soon as Valerie had ascertained Ivy was happy sorting craft supplies with Lara, she sat down heavily on the chair and sighed. She took a couple of minutes to compose herself and let her mind stop racing, then texted Tabitha to tell her she'd arrived. A ping a few moments later alerted her Tabitha had received her message.

'There you go.' Jacob set her latte on the table. 'Anything else?'

'Not for now, Jacob, thanks. What are we making tonight, anyway?'

'Mainly tree decorations, but really anything Lara tells us to.'

She couldn't help smiling at that. Lara was a sweet kid, but single-minded when she was on a mission. She was a good influence on Ivy and not for the first time, Valerie was glad Ivy and Lara were friends, and by extension she and Tabitha.

'Hi.' Tabitha came in, bringing the cold air in with her. 'Wow, I hadn't realised it was that cold.'

'It's meant to get colder still. I see you got some presents.' She nodded to the bag Tabitha was carrying.

'For Lara,' she mouthed, and Valerie made a zipping her lips closed motion.

'Let me drop these in the back and I'll be right out.' Tabitha turned to her brother. 'Can I have a vanilla latte, please?'

At Jacob's incredulous expression, she said, 'Then I'll come help with the craft session, I promise.'

'Fine,' he said, rolling his eyes in mock-exasperation.

Valerie hid a smile. Tabitha and Jacob had always been quite the sibling double act.

When Tabitha returned she said, 'Sorry, Valerie, gimme one sec. I want to say hi to Stanley, and is that Paul with him?'

Valerie craned her neck to see past all the other patrons. It really was very busy. 'Looks like it.'

Valerie watched as Tabitha excused herself for interrupting, then leant down and kissed Stanley's cheek. She said hi to Paul, too, and when she was walking back to her seat, Valerie heard her say to Paul, 'Make sure he behaves himself, eh? He's a total troublemaker. Need to watch him like a hawk.'

Paul and Stanley both laughed and Stanley picked up his stick and tried to tap Tabitha on the back with it, but she was out of range. However, she must have felt the whoosh of air at his attempt as she spun round and shot him a warning look just as Jacob set their drinks in front of them.

Valerie loved the camaraderie Tabitha and Stanley shared. She'd never had that with someone of that age. Well, she didn't exactly know what age he was, but he looked to be ninety something.

'Right, that's that whippersnapper taken care of. How are you?'

Whilst Valerie was recounting the no-show husband tale of woe, the door opened again and Mr McCafferty entered. 'Don't look now, but there's the headmaster.' She leant forward. 'I hope you've been a very good girl this year.'

'Ha ha!' said Tabitha, overbrightly.

Valerie watched as Mr McCafferty looked around

uncertainly then, his eyes alighting on Tabitha, weaved his way through the tables towards them.

'Tabitha, the head's coming your way,' Valerie hissed.

'Hi, Mrs Nicol. I hope you don't mind me joining you. Tabitha said I couldn't miss the craft session, and since I have a little free time, I thought I'd give it a go.'

'Valerie, please. We're not in school now,' she said, smiling.

'Then, it's Fraser.' He nodded to where Lara and Ivy were deep in pom poms, glitter, pine cones and felt. 'The girls seem to be getting a head start.'

'Oh, don't worry, we'll show them how it's done,' said Tabitha. 'We can be quite competitive around here, especially Jacob.'

At the counter, Jacob looked up at mention of his name, and Fraser smiled at him, but Valerie noted the smile didn't quite reach his eyes.

'Ten minutes, Jacob.' Tabitha held up both hands and splayed them in case he hadn't heard her.

Jacob nodded and Tabitha explained the format of the evening to Fraser as Valerie looked on. If she wasn't mistaken there was a frisson of something between her friend and the headmaster. Interesting – and not before time – that Tabitha was keen on someone. And from where she was sitting it didn't seem to be one-way traffic.

'Does anyone want a drink?' Fraser asked.

Valerie and Tabitha gestured to the drinks already in front of them and Fraser said, 'OK. Tabitha, what can you recommend?'

Tabitha thought for a second and then said, 'Peppermint hot chocolate. You do like chocolate, right?'

Fraser smiled and Valerie thought he was quite

attractive when he did so. He must be around her age, so a little, but not much, older than Tabitha. She could see a match here. As his eyes met Tabitha's, on closer inspection, Valerie thought they were almost cobalt. Yep, she could definitely feel a frisson between these two. Was it too early to rub her hands in glee at a possible romantic match? She'd need to collar Tabitha later to find out. She didn't have time now to do much more than raise an eyebrow at Tabitha and gesture in Fraser's direction when he went off to order his drink, but Tabitha laughed her off. Valerie wasn't to be put off that easily; she'd get to the bottom of it soon enough. It wasn't every day your best friend brought the headmaster over to have drinks with you, after all.

As Fraser returned from ordering his drink, he stopped by Paul and Stanley's table and said hi for a minute before he resumed his place at the table with Valerie and Tabitha.

'It seems to be quite the meeting place for Heatherwood,' Fraser said with a smile.

'It's certainly the hub in this part of town,' Valerie agreed.

'Right, I'd best go help Jacob bring all the materials through. You pair can get your thinking caps on about what you're going to make.'

Valerie bit her lip and looked at Fraser, whose eyes crinkled at the corners when he laughed.

'I feel like I'm on trial here,' he said. 'And with Ivy and Lara here, if my efforts aren't up to scratch, I'll be the talk of the school tomorrow.'

'Oh, I think your secret's safe with them. Ivy loves it here. She envies Lara being able to come here whenever she likes.'

'Yes, I suppose her mum and dad owning the place is a

bit of a bonus,' Fraser said.

Valerie scrunched up her forehead. 'Dad?'

Fraser gestured towards Jacob, and Valerie burst out laughing. 'Jacob, Lara's dad. Jacob, Tabitha's husband. Oh, that's too funny. Wait until I tell her.'

'What? You mean they're not married?' Fraser's mouth gaped open slightly.

Valerie shook her head. 'Nope.'

'And he's not Lara's dad?'

'Definitely not, and thank goodness.'

Valerie noted the mix of relief and confusion cross Fraser's features. 'But he's a great guy. Surely he'd be a catch for Tabitha.'

Valerie couldn't retain her composure any longer. 'I'm not arguing with you that Jacob's a great guy, but he's married.'

'Oh!' More confusion was visible on Fraser's face.

Deciding to put him out of his misery, Valerie said, 'He's also Tabitha's brother.'

Fraser's eyes widened and he turned round to survey them rather intently before spinning back to Valerie and saying, 'Now you point that out, it makes a lot of sense.'

She smiled. As he turned back to look at the siblings again, she smiled again. Things were looking up for Tabitha.

Chapter Twelve

'Right, everyone, join any table that has been set up with craft materials. Tabitha is going to walk you through how to make Christmas baubles.' Jacob paused and smiled at Stanley and a middle-aged couple who looked as if they were champing at the bit to start.

'I'll be showing you later how to make edible Christmas decorations,' he said. 'Our assistant, Lara, will be around to help those who need a hand with their tree decorations, and if you need any advice, ask Tabitha.' Everyone laughed. 'No, seriously, you can ask any of us. Are we ready? Then let's craft!'

Immediately, everyone became very animated and industrious-looking. There was even rolling up of sleeves involved.

Fraser glanced over at Tabitha, kicking himself for not realising Jacob was her brother, not her husband, not Lara's dad. He was trying to keep the smile from his face, when his eyes fell upon Lara, busy with Ivy. He tamped down his elation, when he realised little had changed. Tabitha was still a parent of a child at his school. It wasn't as if he could date her, even if she was interested. Yet, somehow knowing she wasn't married or with someone else gave him a tiny ray of hope, or at least it assuaged his guilt at liking her.

Tabitha stopped by the table, arms filled with supplies. 'I need to go and help get everyone organised. Excuse me for a bit, guys.'

'Just you and me then, Fraser. What do you fancy making?' said Valerie.

Fraser shrugged. 'I don't mind. What do you suggest?'

'Hi, Mr McCafferty. Have you done any crafts before?'

Fraser looked at Lara, still in her school uniform, which now seemed to be coated in a surprising amount of glitter, as were her face and hands.

'Clearly not as many as you, Lara.' He indicated her clothing by waving a finger up and down.

She grinned. 'Mum says I like to get into the spirit of things.'

She paused and he realised she was waiting for him to elaborate on his craft capabilities.

'Well, Lara, it has been a long time since I did any proper crafting. Can you suggest something for me to make?'

Lara pursed her lips then said, 'Since it's been a while, why don't you start with something simple, like a bauble? Unless … you're not one of these people who need to have their tree all super-coordinated or anything, are you?'

From her tone, Fraser got the impression that was a bad thing, so he shook his head. 'Oh, no, I like to mix it up a bit.'

Lara's face broke into a broad smile. 'I'll go get you some materials then.'

Fraser shot Valerie a look as Lara set off on her mission and Valerie smirked.

'You don't know what you've let yourself in for. You're about to have a masterclass in bauble creation.'

Fraser laughed, but he stopped short when Lara returned with a basket containing clear baubles, plain white baubles, a variety of sequins in various colours, feathers and ribbons.

'Here you go. Oh, I forgot the glue.' She dashed off and Fraser watched as she was waylaid by Stanley on her return. He marvelled at how the little girl got on so easily with everyone. It was clear to see she spent a lot of time here and was well liked by the café's patrons.

'Mr McCafferty, could you please sit at Stanley's and Mr Fairbairn's table? Stanley wants to make some baubles for his friends, but I think he might need a bit of help or he'll never manage it in time.' She whispered the last part as if she was afraid of risking offending the old man if he overheard. 'Mrs Nicol, Ivy says you're making snowmen gifts with her.'

When Valerie looked bemused, Lara said, 'For her grans and grampas. She told me you were having problems knowing what to get them.'

Valerie flushed and Fraser wondered if there was a story there.

'Right,' Valerie said. 'Lead me to the snowmen.' She glanced at Fraser and mouthed, 'Have fun.'

Fraser pushed out his chair and headed over to the two men. 'Room for a not so little one?'

'Aye, son, sit yourself down. The more the merrier. I'm Stanley.'

'Fraser.' He shook the older man's hand. 'Mr Fairbairn.' He nodded towards him.

'Paul's just fine,' said Mr Fairbairn.

Fraser, wrong-footed for a moment, finally said, 'Good. And in that case, Fraser's fine too.' He smiled and sat down, conscious of the vast age difference between the three of them. He knew Paul was up for retirement and he'd asked not to retire. The issue had also come up in the education authority meeting. They were pushing for him to take retirement. However, Fraser had seen how well respected Paul was in the school, both by staff and pupils, and he'd held out for his janitor continuing past retirement age. He regretted having been a little hard on Paul and wanted to make it up to him, and the rest of the staff for that matter, for not being sweetness and light much of the time, and perhaps coming across as too heavy-handed in many respects, but between the pressure from the council and the emotional impact of having to put his mother in the care home, it had been hard to be more fun and friendly. However, these past few days, he *had* felt a little different, a bit more hopeful.

Maybe there was something to be said for the spirit of the season.

'So, boys, what are we doing with all these bits and pieces? Any ideas?' Stanley asked.

Paul looked at Fraser, perhaps assuming a headmaster would have more of a handle on things than he did. When he looked back at Stanley, he said, 'Well, seeing all these bits and bobs Lara has left us, I'm thinking I might start off with making a robin, something simple, you know?'

'Great idea.' Stanley smiled encouragingly at Paul, then turned to Fraser. 'What about yourself, young Fraser?'

Fraser smiled inwardly. It was a while since anyone had called him 'young Fraser'. He was forty-three, for goodness' sake, but he supposed to Stanley, who had to be more than double his age, he was indeed young Fraser.

He felt a little put on the spot, so simply said, 'I like

Paul's idea.' He noted Paul sit up a little straighter.

'Robins it is, then. Good suggestion, Paul.' Stanley patted the janitor on the arm. 'I may as well do a robin as well.' He looked at Fraser and Paul. 'Well, you've heard of the song "Three Craws Sat Upon a' Wa"? Our baubles can be three robins sat upon a' wa'.' He cackled with laughter and slapped his hand on his trousers, until he was almost wheezing.

'Hey, steady on, Stanley. We don't want you having an episode,' Paul said.

'Oh, wheesht. I'm fine. Right, let's get these robins made.'

The three of them set to work, eyes down, hands busy. Fraser decided to make the bottom of his bauble red for the robin's breast by gluing felt onto it, then he cut out brown felt for the wings and the top half of the robin, before cutting yellow card and folding it in half for the beak, then finished it off with googly eyes.

Stanley had opted for covering the top half of his base bauble in gold glitter, with red glitter on the bottom half. He then had to wait a while for it all to dry, before he added a bronze beak and large felt wings. Personally, Fraser thought they were a little oversized, but it was the thought that counted.

When Fraser next glanced up, he noted Paul had used a blue felt for both the bauble background and for his robins, with only the red of their breasts adding a pop of colour to it. Well, that and the white of the snowy scene he'd set at the bottom and sides.

'Blue, Paul?' Fraser asked, tilting his chin upwards.

'Yeah.' Paul grinned. 'They're freezing. It's brass monkeys out there.'

Stanley guffawed and had tears running down his face. When he composed himself again, he said, 'It's supposed to be three robins replacing the craws on the wa', not brass monkeys.' He burst out laughing again.

Fraser looked on, tickled by the amusement the elderly gent had found in such a simple activity.

When they were finished, Fraser went to get up, but Stanley stayed him with a hand on his arm. 'Not so fast, young man. I need your help and your ideas. I have three baubles to make.'

Fraser sighed inwardly. Much as he was enjoying himself, at this rate, he'd never get up to Bay Park tonight. He checked his watch then said, 'OK, let's do it.'

After much discussion and hilarity, between them they came up with star baubles; silver and red striped baubles, which Fraser thought looked suspiciously like a sofa pattern; reindeer with ribbons on the front of the bauble with antlers made from pipe cleaners; and a snowy scene depicted on one bauble, created with various sizes of silver and white beads, finished off with silver and white ribbon.

When they finally sat back, Fraser had to admit he'd enjoyed himself greatly. Occasionally, he'd caught Tabitha's eye, and she'd stopped by the table a few times to admire their efforts, but largely, he'd had fun both creating something from nothing and having a bit of friendly banter with the two older men.

'Well, I think that deserves a cuppa,' said Stanley as he sat back to take in his creations.

'Hear, hear,' said Paul. 'Who knew crafting was such thirsty work.'

'Jacob, can we have some drinks over here? Look how hard we've worked,' Stanley said, pouting as if he wanted a pat on the head or a prize.

Fraser smothered a smile. He was a wily old fox, and he clearly had Jacob wrapped around his little finger.

'Decaff tea for you, nothing more, at this time of night, or I'll be on a warning,' Jacob said.

Stanley chuckled. 'That's my boy.' Turning to Paul and Fraser, he said, 'I wish he was my boy. He's a godsend.'

Tabitha stopped by the table just then. 'Ooh, someone's been busy. Stanley, do I detect your hand in all of this?' she asked with a smile, her hand resting gently on the old man's shoulder.

'Indeed you do, Tabitha, but I can't take all the credit. Paul and Fraser have done a grand job.'

'And who, may I ask, will be the proud recipients of tonight's baubles?' she asked.

'Well, mine are for my friends Wullie, Jimmy and Una at the care home. I've been palled up wi' Wullie and Jimmy for years.' He paused. 'Una hasn't been there long, but I feel as if I've known her half my life.'

Fraser stared. It couldn't be.

'Stanley, what care home are you at?'

'Bay Park, son. You know, the one up on the lochside.'

Fraser nodded. 'Yes, I do know it. My mum's there.'

He noticed Tabitha's glance at him, but he was too taken aback at the coincidence Stanley had just revealed to do more than register it.

'Oh, really? What's her name? I probably know her.'

'I think you probably do, Stanley. Her name's Una. Una McCafferty.'

'Oh my goodness, you're Una's boy. I can't believe it. Wait til I tell her. She's always going on about you, how proud she is of you, how good a son you are.' He paused.

'Sorry, son, I didn't mean to embarrass you. Suffice to say, she loves you very much and appreciates everything you do for her.'

Again Fraser was aware of Tabitha's eyes on him.

'Does she play chess with you?' Stanley asked.

'Yes.' Fraser laughed. 'And she usually beats me.'

Stanley put his hand on top of Fraser's. 'Don't take it personally, son. She usually beats me too.' He turned to Tabitha, and then Jacob, who arrived with his tea. 'Jacob, Tabitha, can you believe Fraser's mum is one of my best buddies? I made a bauble for her.' He held up the silver and white snowy beaded bauble. 'Do you think she'll like it?'

Fraser, a lump in his throat, said, 'I know she'll love it.'

Stanley's face lit up and then he put a hand over his mouth. 'Jacob, how much time do we have?'

Jacob smiled. 'Don't worry. You still have time, although at one point I thought I was going to have to hurry you along, as you guys were chatting away like there was no tomorrow.'

Stanley laughed. 'Well, when you're my age, there might not be a tomorrow,' he said to Jacob's retreating back.

Fraser smirked. Stanley was a riot. A thought struck him. 'Stanley, are you heading back to Bay Park tonight?'

'Yes, Jacob takes me back once he, Tabitha and Lara have tidied up.'

'Well, if you want, and you'd rather go sooner, I'm heading up there to visit Mum, but I need to go like in ten minutes, or visiting time will be finished.'

'Oh, that would be great, son. Very kind. Let me say goodbye and thanks to Jacob.'

As Stanley spoke with Jacob, Paul whispered to Fraser,

'I think you have a fan.'

Fraser smiled. 'No, I think my mum has a fan.'

Paul chuckled. 'That too. So, what are you going to do with your baubles?'

'I'm not sure. I wasn't going to bother putting up a tree this year, but…'

Lara materialised by his side, a look of horror on her face. 'But, sir, you have to put up a tree. Where will Santa leave your presents otherwise?'

'She has a point, sir,' Paul said, a smile on his lips.

Fraser, beaten, said, 'OK, Lara, you've convinced me. I'll put up a tree.'

Lara eyed him carefully. 'Promise?'

Trying to hold in his laughter, Fraser said, 'I promise.'

'What have you signed up for, Fraser?' Jacob asked as he removed their cups and tidied their table.

'To put my tree up. Lara's appalled that I wasn't intending to put one up.'

'Quite right, that's shocking!' Jacob said, his lips nudging upwards. 'For a moment there I thought she'd signed you up for the Santa race.'

Fraser screwed up his face. 'Santa race?'

'Yes, Santa race.' Stanley nudged him. 'You must know about the Santa race. It's famous and it's for charity. People come from all over to watch it.'

'From all over where?' Fraser said.

'Loch Lomond,' said Stanley as if it were the size of the United States. He lowered his voice slightly. 'Some even come from Edinburgh.'

'I'm not much of a runner,' said Fraser.

'Neither am I,' chipped in Paul, 'but I do it.'

Fraser's eyes widened. 'You do a Santa race?'

Paul chuckled. 'You don't need to look so shocked.'

'No, no…' Fraser started.

Paul raised his hand to stop him. 'I'm only kidding, but I do take part in the race. It's good fun. You should do it.'

Fraser cast his eyes round the room. Tabitha, Lara, Jacob, Stanley and Paul were all looking at him expectantly. 'OK, fine. Nothing like a bit of peer pressure to get you roped in to something.'

'That's the spirit,' said Jacob. 'Seriously, it's fun. We even have Gluhwein at the end. One of the sponsors provides it.'

'And it's for charity, you say?' Fraser prodded.

'Yep, you choose the charity.'

Straightaway Fraser knew who his charity would be; what he had less of an idea of was who would sponsor him. When he raised that point, voices all around him said, 'I'll sponsor you. Sure, who doesn't want to see the headteacher running in a Santa suit?'

Fraser covered his eyes with his hand. 'I'm never going to live this down, am I? And I haven't even done it yet.'

'You'll be fine, son. It'll be grand. Maybe we could even get your mum to come and watch,' Stanley said.

At Fraser's horrified expression, the whole table burst out laughing. However, despite the potential for humiliation, he felt a warm glow inside and was thankful for the camaraderie Sugar and Spice had provided him with that evening.

Chapter Thirteen

'Your mum is a wonderful woman,' said Stanley as he sat in the passenger seat on their twenty-minute drive to Loch Lomond.

'Can't argue with you there,' said Fraser.

'She really buoys everyone up, you know that?'

Fraser glanced across at him, careful to keep one eye on the road. In the dark, with snow on the windy roads taking them up and along the banks of Loch Lomond, he couldn't be too careful.

'How do you mean?' Fraser asked.

Stanley was quiet for a moment then said, 'Well, whenever anyone is sad, she's the first person many turn to. And she goes out of her way to make newcomers welcome. She has a lot of patience.'

Fraser smiled as he thought of the patience his mum had shown with him over the years, particularly after his dad died, when he knew he'd been a bit of a tearaway. He'd been far from headteacher material then.

'Yes, that sounds like Mum.' His throat constricted. He was looking forward to seeing her and unveiling his surprise in the form of his new friend. He knew she'd be delighted – she believed in serendipity.

As he drew into Bay Park's car park, the snow began to

fall again, gently at first, but by the time he had parked and helped Stanley out of the car, big, fat flakes were falling in a steadier rhythm, blanketing the car park around them. With the backdrop of the loch behind them, illuminated by the care home's lights, it looked truly magical.

'I can't wait to see her face,' said Stanley, and somehow Fraser didn't think he meant just at the surprised look on it. No, Stanley's face lit up when he spoke of Fraser's mother. Were they too old for romance? And if they weren't, did that mean there was still hope for him?

'Hi, Mum, sorry I'm a bit late.'

'Oh, Fraser, darling, it's good to see you. I did wonder if you'd make it with the weather.'

He bent to kiss her cheek. 'Yes, well, I did ask myself that, too, but luckily the snow went off again, and has only just come back on.'

'So, how's things? How's work? How's your love life?'

'OK. Not bad. Better than it was,' Fraser replied, used to his mum's rat-a-tat fashion of asking him questions.

A frown crossed her face and he could tell she was processing his comment regarding his love life, so he hurried on. 'You know, the funniest thing happened tonight.'

'Oh?' she said, one eyebrow raised.

'I bumped into a friend of yours.' Fraser was enjoying the puzzlement crossing her features.

'Who was it? Where did you meet them…?'

Before she could ask any further questions, he decided to put her out of her misery. Stanley had been standing just round the corner and Fraser said, 'You'd better come out now.'

Fraser's mum's brow creased again, like she was lost once more as to what was happening. But her face lit up when she spotted Stanley, and Fraser knew straightaway that the admiration Stanley felt for Fraser's mum was reciprocated.

'Stanley, you old devil! I was wondering where you'd got to.'

'Hi, Una. I was down at Sugar and Spice.' He creaked his way into the armchair beside her. 'Did you not see young Jacob come and pick me up earlier?'

Fraser's mum tilted her head to the side then said, 'That's right. You were going to a craft event at the café.'

'Bingo! And guess who I bumped into there.' He raised his stick slightly and pointed at Fraser.

Fraser's mum turned to him. 'You were at a craft workshop?' The incredulity in her voice made Fraser laugh.

'Yes, Mum, I was at a craft workshop.'

'How did…? I couldn't even get you to do crafts when you were a wee boy.'

Fraser grinned. 'Ah, sometimes there are some very persuasive people out there.'

Stanley laughed. 'I'll say. He's just signed up to do the Santa race, and me and you are going to watch him.'

Fraser's mum swung her gaze between him and Stanley, as if unsure whether Stanley was winding her up or not.

'I have, in case you're wondering,' Fraser confirmed.

'Wondering? What I'm wondering is, who kidnapped my son? Not that I didn't love the old one, but this seems like a new and improved version. A more relaxed version.'

'This calls for a cup of tea,' said Stanley.

Fraser laughed, wondering how many drinks Stanley had per day. He had to be up half the night at the toilet.

'Una, I almost forgot. I have a wee something for you.' Stanley pulled the bauble out of the little box Jacob had given him to keep it in, and passed it to her. 'For your tree.'

'Oh, Stanley, it's beautiful.' And as she admired it and turned it in her hands, then held it up to the light, it seemed to shimmer and sparkle.

'I'm glad you like it. It's a magic bauble, for a magic person.'

'Oh, you.' Fraser's mum nudged him with her shoulder.

Fraser sat drinking his tea, listening to the banter between Stanley and his mother, and a warm glow suffused his insides: happiness. He felt truly happy, for the first time in a long while.

When it came time for him to leave, he planted a kiss on his mum's cheek and gave Stanley a hug.

'If I don't see you beforehand, Stanley, I'll see you at the Santa race. Sure you don't want to have a go yourself? You're not going to try to pretend you're too old for it, are you? Not that old chestnut.'

'Away with you!' said Stanley.

Fraser grinned. 'Mum could push you round in a wheelchair.'

'No, Fraser. Me and your mum will sit by the finish line with a nice hot chocolate.'

'Cushy number if you can get it.' He patted Stanley on the arm. 'I really enjoyed tonight. Thanks for making it so fun.'

'My pleasure, son. And you know something I've learned over my ninety-four years?'

'What?' said Fraser as he helped Stanley up out of his chair.

'There really are no coincidences. Fate has a way of playing its hand.'

As Fraser was mulling over what Stanley meant, his mum said, 'Is that your bag, Fraser?'

'Oh, Mum, sorry. It's for you. I was in T&J's and picked up some books I thought you'd like.'

His mum reached up to touch his cheek. 'That was very kind of you. Thank you.'

'You're welcome. Remember to keep your phone charged so I can message you. I'd best get back. This snow's falling even faster now.'

The three of them looked out of the window and agreed it was best if he made a move.

As Fraser drove back from Bay Park, his thoughts turned to the evening's events. Funnily enough, he'd have no problem keeping his promise to Lara about putting up his tree. Little by little his Christmas spirit was returning.

Chapter Fourteen

'Munro, can you get the door, please?' Valerie called the next morning. The chime of the doorbell sounded again. It was likely the postman, but she couldn't exactly stop feeding the twins from where she was reclined in bed.

'Munro!' She was going to give herself a coronary if she continued like this. Where was the blasted man? He'd dropped Ivy at school, deigning to do a parental task for a change and had been due back ages ago, but she hadn't heard him return. She'd have to let the postman or courier or whoever it was leave the package in the porch. She hated doing that as she always liked to check it wasn't damaged, particularly at this time of year, when parcels tended to get roughed up a bit, from couriers being under a lot of pressure to deliver a lot of parcels in a very short space of time.

Fifteen minutes later, she put the twins down for a nap and went to have a shower. If Munro was in the house, she was none the wiser, but she couldn't be bothered going all the way back downstairs to check. Time was at a premium and right now, getting a shower, allowing the hot jets to cascade over her tired, exhausted body, was far more important than checking if her husband had returned from school drop-off.

The zen feeling that had enveloped her after she'd spent a good chunk of quality time with Ivy the night before and chatting with friends old and new, sharing Christmas stories – how they'd be spending Christmas, who they'd be spending Christmas with, what the children wanted from Santa – had evaporated as her husband's thoughtlessness once again made her blood pressure rise.

As the water flowed over her, she kept repeating to herself the mantra she'd lived by for a long time: I cannot be responsible for other people's actions, but I can decide if and how I let them affect me. She didn't want Munro's obliviousness to undo all the good work of the night before. She knew being stressed not only wasn't good for her, but it wasn't good for the twins, and it certainly wasn't good for Ivy. Coming out of the shower, she breathed a sigh of relief when she saw the twins were still fast asleep. She stood over the Moses baskets, marvelling at how perfect her babies were. Unbelievably tiny, both only around the five-pound mark when they were born, with Poppy a couple of ounces heavier than her brother. When they were asleep like this, she could watch them for hours, and she remained in awe of the fact she had given birth to them. They were part of her, her and Munro. Shame he didn't seem to realise that the workload that went with having twins also fell partly to him. She knew, from experience with Ivy, that the exhaustion phase passed, but sometimes she was so tired she couldn't even think straight.

The door slammed as Valerie was towel-drying her hair. For goodness' sake. How many times had she told Munro not to slam the door? It was annoying enough anyway, but triply so when you had newborn twins who were prone to wake from a nap at the slightest sound. She gritted her teeth and padded downstairs in her dressing gown.

'Oh, hi,' Munro said, putting a pod in the coffee machine and sorting himself a cup. 'Want one?'

Valerie nodded. 'Yes, please.' She really wanted a fully caffeinated coffee, but that was a no-go whilst she was breast-feeding, and therefore out of bounds for the next eight to ten months anyway. Another sacrifice she'd had to make that Munro hadn't.

'Munro, can you remember not to slam the door when you come in, please? You could have woken the twins.'

'Huh?' he said distractedly. 'Yeah, sure.' He finished making them both coffee then passed Valerie hers.

'So, what kept you? I thought you'd have been back from drop-off ages ago.' Valerie took a sip of her coffee.

'Oh, I went to the gym. Figured it was a good time.'

What about her going to the gym, or even getting fifteen minutes to herself, where she wasn't expected to do laundry or pay bills or run errands with twins in tow?

'Hmm,' she said noncommittally.

'Listen, hon, I need to speak to you about something.' Munro set his coffee on the marble worktop.

'OK. I'm listening.'

He looked down at the floor then raised his gaze to Valerie. 'You know how there has been talk of a merger between Dynamic Innovation and Key Quest?'

Valerie frowned. 'Yes?' Where was he going with this?

Munro pulled at his bottom lip, something he did when he was nervous. 'Well, they want a meeting.'

'OK? And?'

He shifted closer to her. She knew the move. It was one he used to use to placate her when he knew she wouldn't like what he had to say. She moved back a little.

'Spit it out, Munro.'

His jaw tensed. 'Fine. They've arranged a meeting for the twenty-third.'

Valerie gaped. 'I hope you said no. That's too close to Christmas. And you know what flights from London are like then. Heathrow's always chaotic and that 7 a.m. flight down on the twenty-third will be chock a block.'

He blew out a breath. 'Val, the meeting's not in London.' He sighed. 'It's in San Francisco.'

'No,' Valerie said quietly. 'No, no, no, no, no.' Her hands balled into fists as she fought to maintain control. 'Munro, you are not leaving me all alone at Christmas with our daughter and twins for a business meeting that could easily happen after Christmas.'

He shook his head. 'Honey, I've tried to renegotiate the date, but there was no other date everyone else could make.'

'Munro, you need to start putting this family first. There is only one of me. You don't get it. I am absolutely exhausted.' She was shouting now. She couldn't help it. 'And you don't see that. You bog off to the gym, the gym! I wish I could bog off somewhere. And now you're bogging off to a meeting in bloomin' San Francisco two days before Christmas? Are you for real?'

'Actually, I need to go on the twenty-first to prepare for the meeting. There are various departments flying in.'

'Aaargh! Munro, look around you. We need you! I need you, and if you can't see that and do something about it, then go to California, attend your precious business meeting, but don't expect me to like it and don't expect things to be the same between us once you get back.'

She picked up her bag from the kitchen table just as one, or both, of the twins started wailing.

'It's *my* gym time, *honey*. The twins have been fed, fortunately. Why don't you go look after the children you helped create? I'll pick Ivy up later. There's expressed milk in the fridge. Since you don't know, the twins' next feed is in two hours.'

'But Val, you can't go.' Panic laced his voice and for a moment she felt a twinge of satisfaction. The twins wouldn't come to any harm under his care, she hoped. Plus, she had a nanny cam. She'd check on him from Sugar and Spice. That had been her zen place the night before. She was sure she could have a nice breakfast there, maybe some pancakes or something, or one of Jacob's Christmas-themed cakes.

'Sorry? I can't go?'

'You can't just leave me,' he whined.

'Really? But you can leave me, leave us, and traipse off to San Francisco? Yeah, double standards much? See you later, Munro. And remember to change the twins' nappies. You do remember how, don't you?'

She strode out of the front door without a backward glance, reversed her car out of the driveway, aware of his eyes on her as she left the street. She sincerely hoped he dealt with the twins soon. They only increased in volume if left to cry.

'Amy!' Bella caught up with her friend as she pulled on her padded jacket. She may not be quite as warm as Amy, who was wearing an ankle-length coat, but she'd be able to run better.

Amy grinned. 'You ready for this?'

'I'll have to be, won't I? Whose idea was this again?' she

grumbled.

'Ha! Yours.' She pushed the door open ahead of them and they rejoined the children and other teachers in the playground.

The parent-teacher association had contributed to the purchase of some of the equipment and had helped Paul set things up for today, and the children themselves had been so excited about the winter version of sports day that her whole class had happily mucked in. Some of them had even been counting down the days. Bella figured from a child's perspective, it certainly beat doing fractions and multiplication, even if she had tried to jazz up maths with the involvement of Santa hats, candy canes and gingerbread men sums.

Today, the whole school had timed slots for taking part in the winter games. She prayed the weather would stay fine. Paul would start them off on the jingle bell jog, where the children, and teachers, would run round the trim trail wearing Santa hats with bells on, hence the name. Then they'd line up on the football pitch and race each other in the reindeer sack race – each participant had to be sporting antlers. If they reached the finish line antler-less they would be disqualified, although if their antlers fell off, they could jump back whilst still in their sack to retrieve them. This had been a favourite of the boys in her class.

'Miss, miss!' Ivy Nicol was walking towards Bella. 'When are the relay races? Mrs Dalwood said Lara and I have to bring back the Christmas tree costumes for the next group to wear.'

Bella looked at her watch. 'In about half an hour, Ivy. Do you want me to come find you when it's time?'

Ivy's face lit up and Bella noted her eyes were the same

sapphire blue as her mother's. Poor woman had seemed very stressed last time she'd seen her. Despite being wrapped up in her own misery, she'd noticed Ivy's mum, and she wondered if it was one injured soul recognising another. She was probably imagining it.

'Yes, please, miss.' Ivy broke into Bella's thoughts and Bella smiled at her, and Lara, who was muttering under her breath. Lara's eyes had been shining as if she'd been laughing at something, or as if she'd been part of a great in-joke.

The girls ran off and Bella was left wondering who was rotating the other costumes, if the girls had been put in charge of these, since she knew there were Christmas puddings, snowflakes and giant candy cane outfits too. Each team would start with a Christmas tree, with the snowflake in second position, the candy cane on the third leg, then the Christmas puddings would run the anchor leg.

At least the Christmas puddings have more padding, thought Bella. If there's a mad last-minute dash over the line, they could always bounce off each other.

But the pièce de résistance was that planned by the upper school children themselves – the Christmas obstacle course. It was a disaster waiting to happen and had such a diverse set of elements, it could only end in total carnage, but it would be fun to watch, although perhaps not to actively participate in. Only two of the teachers had been allowed to see it so far, the rest of them having to wait until the great unveiling. Bella wasn't one of the chosen few, but had gleaned snippets from her class's excited chatter over the past couple of weeks.

'You ready for the teachers' race later?' asked Amy.

'Yeah. I'm not doing that,' Bella said.

Amy screwed up her face. 'Oh, yes you are. You do know your class, and mine, and every other class here, lives for this moment – when we make total prats of ourselves?'

'Maybe, but not this year,' Bella said, slipping her hands inside her pockets and surveying the playground filled with every possible Christmas idea known to mankind. It almost felt as if a Christmas fairy had asked the children what they wished for, then granted each and every one of their very different wishes.

Paul was standing next to the head, holding a bullhorn, and they were laughing together. Bella couldn't believe her eyes. She'd had the distinct impression they didn't get on. Mr McCafferty was always so staid, but today his eyes were crinkling at the corners. Maybe he liked sports or perhaps he was a big fan of Christmas. Whatever it was, she was delighted to see the change in him. He was even quite handsome when he smiled, not that she was interested. Funny, she'd never thought about whether he was married or not. But then he hadn't exactly invited conversation with her, or any of the staff, plus he didn't come into the staffroom very often. He was much more of a hands-off headteacher than their previous head, Kathleen Russell, who was now on mat leave, and mum to baby Charlotte, who'd now be around three months old. She'd be celebrating her first Christmas shortly.

Bella felt another pang at the thought that avenue was closed to her for now, that she wouldn't be the one being pregnant then having a bouncing, gummy baby anytime soon. She wondered if she'd ever meet someone else she loved enough to have a child with. She'd certainly find it harder to trust in the future. Relationships were an investment, but what was the point if they could be smashed to pieces in a matter of moments, or a couple of conversations?

'Miss?'

Bella looked down to see one of the primary twos peeping out over the edge of their sack. He was so little she could almost see nothing except his eyes. Were it not for the lopsided antlers, or the voice, she might not have known there was a child in the sack at all.

'Yes, sweetheart.' She couldn't for the life of her remember the boy's name.

'Could you fix my antlers, please? They keep falling down.' His trembling lip showed his frustration and she decided now was not the time to be feeling sorry for herself. These kids needed her. They didn't need her half-hearted attempt to embrace Christmas; they needed her to be fully in the Christmas spirit with them. She'd have time enough later to wallow if that's what she wanted, but right now, her role was clear. She had to help the kids have the best winter-themed sports day ever.

'Paul, have you done any training for this Santa race?' Fraser asked as they paced the playground making sure everything was as it should be, righting pieces of equipment that had been knocked over and picking up pieces that had to be returned to start lines.

Paul turned to him. 'Nope. In fact, I'm hoping my body doesn't give up on me so I don't make a holy show of myself.'

'I'll stick with you then. We can look pathetic

together.'

A wave of contentment fell over Paul. It had felt good to gel with the younger man, even if it was over something as innocuous as a Santa race, and it was always good fun. Half the schoolchildren came to watch; even previous pupils came to cheer them on. This year he was running for a local cancer charity.

'Fraser, are you doing the race for charity?' Paul asked.

'I thought I might try to raise funds for the folks up at Bay Park.'

'That's a great idea. Wasn't that funny about your mum and Stanley knowing each other?' For a second, Paul thought of how they could have known if only Fraser had opened up to him or any of the staff before, as he had known Stanley was at Bay Park and could have told him, but no matter; all was well that ended well.

'Yes. And I couldn't believe how good friends they are. They have chess breakfasts.' He leant in conspiratorially. 'I have it on good authority Mum often wins.'

'I play a bit of chess, myself,' Paul said. 'I was chess champion in primary six. Beat forty-eight other children.'

Fraser laughed. 'That's very specific.'

Paul drew himself up and puffed out his chest. 'I'll have you know that was quite the achievement.' He grinned. 'I peaked early, though. I haven't won anything much since.'

'Nothing?' Fraser said, raising an eyebrow.

'Well, a tenner on the lottery, that's about it.'

Fraser laughed and said, 'Right, let's focus. We can continue our Santa race training chat later. We need to ensure no one needs carted off to A&E at this obstacle course.'

Paul smirked. 'They really were quite inventive with it.'

'Oh, I'll bet. I remember being a ten-year-old boy.'

'Yeah, my memory's not quite that good. I have a lot further back to go than you.'

They both laughed and then Paul rolled his eyes at an incoming child. 'Here we go, first casualty. Damian, what happened?'

'I fell. I'm soaked through. Mrs Dalwood said to come see you about getting a change of clothes from lost property.'

'Right, come with me.' Paul shook his head at Fraser as the boy turned towards the school. 'I'll leave you to it. Maybe you should have a go.' He pointed to the obstacle course.

'I think I'll pass.'

Paul smirked as he followed Damian into the school building. Things were looking up. He'd been absolutely flabbergasted when Fraser had come to sit with him and Stanley at the craft night in Sugar and Spice, but equally he'd been taken aback by how well they had got on. Maybe it was simply a case of removing themselves from the school setting, but he wondered if it was more than that. Fraser had looked so delighted when he'd discovered Stanley and his mother were friends. It was almost a relief. Perhaps he was worrying about his mum being in the care home. It would only be natural.

Work may have been looking brighter for the foreseeable future, but he still had to contend with the issues with Elaine. At home, things had been chillier than an Arctic wind, ever since their argument the other night about him retiring, or not retiring.

He sighed. His wife really knew how to hold a grudge, but he didn't want to argue; he wanted to enjoy the festivities. She'd been positively monosyllabic the past few days, and even when he'd told her how successful the craft night had been, how he'd spent the evening in the headmaster's company and discovered the man's mother was in the same care home as Stanley, she'd shown little interest, which wasn't like her. Elaine loved people and gossip.

The Elaine problem would have to wait for another day. For now, his task was to find suitable clothing for a ten-year-old boy who looked thoroughly miserable.

'Right, Damian, let's see what we have for you.'

As they sifted through the lost property together, Paul joked with the young boy, and when he'd despatched him to change, the sole thought that remained with Paul was *I'm needed here. I'm making the right decision not retiring early.* And nothing and no one would make him change his mind, not even his moody wife. For once, she wouldn't get her own way.

Chapter Fifteen

Bella found the weekends were the worst. And with only two more weekends before Christmas, things wouldn't improve anytime soon. At least she had Mac. As if sensing she was thinking about him, Mac barked and rushed over to her, then settled himself down in the basket she'd made of her legs whilst wrapping presents. She didn't even care that he'd crushed the wrapping paper; there were far more important things in life. Like working out what to do with her future, and how to go on without the man she thought she'd spend the rest of her life with.

This year she'd found little joy in the present buying. It wasn't the same. Of course, she still tried to find something for her friends and family that they would like, but it wasn't quite the same as going all-out to find the perfect something for that special person in your life, and Ryan had been that special person in her life for six years.

Normally, this was the only time of year Bella watched romantic films, bingeing all the Hallmark Christmas movies, in place of her usual choices of action and adventure, and sci-fi films. But this year, she couldn't bring herself to watch a single Christmas film and instead had been rewatching her favourite science fiction movies on a loop. Even some of those featured happy couples, but there was more than enough death, and destruction of planets to keep her happy, rather than smiling newlyweds, or worse, couples with newborns.

She was wrapping a pair of tartan flannel pyjamas and a silk dressing gown for her mum when the phone rang.

'Hi, Bella, it's just me. Mum.'

She always said that, as if Bella wouldn't recognise her voice.

'Hi, Mum. What are you up to?'

'Actually, I'm about to go into town for some lunch with a friend. What about you? Any plans this weekend?'

She couldn't exactly tell her mother that, after she'd finished wrapping her Christmas presents, her weekend involved the decimation of other species. Instead she said, 'I might go to the cinema.'

'Oh, that sounds nice. What's on?'

Unsure if her mother was trying to catch her out, Bella said, 'No idea. Might take pot luck.'

'You daredevil,' her mum teased. 'So…'

'Yeah?'

'Are you coming here for Christmas dinner, or do you think there's a chance–?'

'Yes, I'm coming,' Bella said quickly. 'Actually, Mum, I really want to get this finished and I know you're going out for lunch. I'll give you a buzz tomorrow, OK?'

'You could call him, you know.'

When Bella didn't say anything, her mum said, 'Listen, love, don't let him slip through your fingers too easily, will you?'

Bella massaged her temples with her fingers. 'Mum, please. This is hard enough. Ryan doesn't want to be married to me any more.' She broke off as a sob burst from her throat. Saying it out loud sounded so much worse, and always caught her off guard. 'So, can you please just leave it? And yes, I'd really like to come to you for Christmas.'

'OK, don't upset yourself. I was only–'

'I know, Mum, believe me, I know, but it's not helping.'

'Sorry, love. Right, enjoy the film and I'll catch up with you in the week.'

Bella placed her phone back on the table then rested her head on the glass tabletop. Would this ever get any easier?

Fraser laughed at Stanley's joke then raised his eyes to look out over the loch, which was coated in a layer of thick ice. No snow so far today, but when he'd left the house it had been bitterly cold.

He'd decided to visit his mum at the care home earlier in the day as Stanley had challenged him to a game of chess, and he was meeting Paul later.

After the festive sports day, Paul had suggested they go running together, to see if they could last the pace for the upcoming Santa race. Fraser had been surprised at the happiness coursing through him at the simple invitation. It really did feel as if barriers were coming down, barriers he had unwittingly created. It wasn't as if he was standoffish normally, and he hated that he may have given off that vibe, but it seemed the tide was turning. He'd seen at the festive sports day how the teachers had gaped when he'd competed in the teachers' race and come second. Miss McGarry was first. She also used to run for Scotland, a fact she'd neglected to mention until after the race. Still, he'd been happy with his second place, and delighted at his staff's reaction to his participation. He'd noticed Mrs Dalwood railroading Mrs Hopkins into racing and in the end they'd both crossed the line not long after him.

He glanced at his watch. It would be time to make a move soon, but he grinned as Stanley tried to outmanoeuvre his mum at chess. He'd lost to Stanley twenty minutes earlier. Now it was his mum's turn to face the old shark. They were quite evenly matched though. Fraser took a moment to revel in his mum's obvious contentment with her situation here at Bay Park. She was thriving here, and so was Stanley.

Fraser sighed deeply as a wave of relief washed over him. He felt lighter, as if he'd been released from a heavy obligation – not that he saw his mum as an obligation, but it was his job to make sure she was OK, and recently he'd felt a failure in that regard; now, he'd regained confidence from the knowledge she was slotting in nicely at Bay Park and making friends.

Tabitha set her handbag down on the other vacant chair beside Valerie. 'Sorry I'm late. I had masses of parcels to post. I know I should be grateful I've had so many orders, but did they really have to be at the last minute?'

'Sit down and relax,' said Valerie.

Tabitha flumped into the chair. 'I'm so glad we're getting a chance to catch up on our own.'

'Doesn't happen very often,' Valerie said with a wry smile.

'Indeed it does not. This calls for one of Jacob's most luxurious hot chocolates. You in?'

'Does Santa Claus come on Christmas Eve?' Valerie said.

Tabitha grinned and waved her brother over. After he chatted with Valerie for a moment, he went about the task of preparing their drinks.

'Where's Lara today?'

'Oh, she's at a screening of *The Grinch* with her friend Abigail.'

Valerie's eyes widened. 'My God, we really do have the afternoon to ourselves.'

'I know. It's weird. Do you think Munro will cope with the kids?'

'He'll have to. He has this idea he's going to manage to work whilst the twins nap and Ivy will colour in or watch TV or something, but he's in for a shock. All three kids are considerably more demanding than that.'

Tabitha turned to her brother, who arrived with their hot chocolates, which were overflowing with whipped cream and had marshmallows both on top and round the edge of the saucer.

'Thanks, Jacob. You're a star. How's Sophie doing?' She gestured to her sister-in-law, who was more at home in her director job these days than she was behind the counter serving cakes and drinks, but she liked to muck in at the weekends and during busy periods. She said she loved the camaraderie and mixing with all the local people.

Jacob glanced back at his wife then returned his attention to his sister. 'Loving it. Says she's really enjoying being back in the thick of things, and of course, payment in cakes always goes down well.'

Tabitha laughed and Valerie smiled at the easy relationship they had. She'd once felt she had that easy relationship with her husband, and her husband had once looked at her in the same way Jacob was looking at Sophie – adoringly – even after ten years.

Their exchanges had been clipped the past few days, after she'd run out on him and sought solace in this very café. She wouldn't say it had made a huge difference to his behaviour, but when she'd told him she'd only returned for the twins and Ivy, he'd taken a step backwards and she'd registered the shock on his face.

He had unwittingly admitted to finding it hard to settle both twins and had struggled with bottle-feeding them. She'd also found the evidence of five mangled nappies – tapes ripped off. He'd either been distracted when he'd been changing their nappies, or had made a hash of it a few times. Yes, a little humility wouldn't go amiss where her husband was concerned. He needed to remember she was his equal in her work life, too, and although she didn't have quite the same earning power, that had been a choice they'd made together, so she wouldn't allow him to sideline her. There was nothing wrong with wanting to be a stay-at-home parent, but that wasn't for her, and she'd always been under the impression her husband had understood that, until the twins arrived. With three times as many children to look after, and the two teeny ones being, understandably, very demanding of her time, she didn't think it was too much to expect Munro to pick Ivy up from school on the days he finished early, or for him to run the hoover across the living room floor, or clean one of the five toilets they had. He'd wanted the big house; well, it didn't clean itself.

'So, Valerie,' Tabitha said, 'what do you think?'

'Sorry. I was miles away.'

'Don't worry. Still having issues with Munro?'

Valerie nodded. 'He has a meeting in San Francisco on the twenty-third.'

'No way!' Tabitha's mouth fell open, but she quickly corrected her expression. 'And how do you feel about that?'

Valerie shook her head. 'I'm furious, but what can I do? I told him if he goes, he shouldn't expect things to be the same between us when he gets back. If that's not a big enough sign, I don't know what is.'

'Hmm. Or–' Tabitha drummed her fingers on the table for a second '–you could go with him. Have Christmas in San Francisco.'

Valerie's spirits soared for a second and she fidgeted in her chair, straightening. 'Yeah … no, that'd never work. Ivy would be terrified Santa wouldn't know where to find us.'

'Ah, yeah, I hadn't thought of that,' said Tabitha. 'Sorry.'

'Don't be. You were trying to find a solution, which seems a lot more than my husband is doing.'

'Anyway, I have something that will hopefully cheer you up a little.'

'Oh?' Valerie screwed up her face.

'Yes. I remember you saying you didn't have any Christmas-themed jewellery, so I have an early Christmas present for you.'

'You didn't need to do that,' said Valerie as Tabitha passed her a red and gold Tabitha's Trinkets gift box.

'I wanted to,' said Tabitha as Valerie opened the box and withdrew the sparkly fused glass Christmas tree drop earrings.

'Oh, Tabitha, they're adorable. I love them.' Valerie stood up and leant over to embrace her.

When she sat back down, Tabitha said, 'Why don't you put them on now? Maybe they'll help you find your Christmas spirit.'

Personally, Valerie thought it would take more than her friend's gift to pull off that feat, but she appreciated the gesture and she was more than willing to try.

Paul pulled up next to the bench and flopped onto it. Fraser followed suit. Once they'd drunk a good portion of what remained in their water bottles, Paul spoke.

'I'm glad we did this. I'm more out of shape than I thought,' he said.

'You and me both.' Fraser's face was scarlet and his breathing was still laboured. 'You're giving me a showing-up. You must be what, twenty years older than me, and you were running rings round me.'

Paul grinned. 'Almost literally.'

'Thanks. You weren't meant to agree with me,' said Fraser.

'I was brought up not to tell lies,' Paul said with a smile on his face.

'I was brought up to spare people's feelings.'

They both chuckled then Fraser said, 'Oh no, I've just realised something.'

'What?'

'I don't have a Santa suit, and the race is in less than a week. Where am I going to find one?'

Paul dismissed his concerns with a wave of his hand. 'It's fine. I'll lend you one.'

Fraser's face screwed up. 'What will *you* wear then?'

'I'll still have a suit. I'll lend you my spare suit.'

'You have a spare Santa suit?' Fraser's eyes widened.

Paul burst out laughing. 'Yes. This isn't my first rodeo, you know.'

'Or your first Santa race, obviously.' Fraser shook his head. 'A spare Santa suit. You're full of surprises, Paul.'

'I like to think so,' he said with a wink.

Paul stretched, and cracked his back. Oh, he was stiff. The hot shower after that run had helped, but he wasn't getting any younger, and he'd been determined to keep pace with Fraser. He smiled at the thought that just over a week ago he'd have referred to him as the head or the headmaster, and now they were on first-name terms and going running together. How things had changed. And he hadn't been able to prevent himself from pushing himself whilst running. There was most definitely life left in the old dog yet.

He was looking forward to Christmas a little more, what with the Santa race coming up the following week, but he knew he really had to get things back on track with Elaine, and she wasn't an easy woman to win round. She was too used to getting her own way. That was the problem with falling for a strong woman – they were not only strong-minded but strong-willed too.

She was out Christmas shopping – again. He was beginning to wonder if she should become a professional shopper; she certainly did enough shopping. So, once he'd ascertained she wouldn't be back for a while, he'd set to work, grabbing his laptop and researching cruises for over Easter break. If he managed to get a good price, then maybe she wouldn't be able to berate him or find fault with him not retiring. He'd compared the cruises he'd found against the one she'd suggested, as he knew his wife was nothing if not meticulous, and she would have gone for maximum comfort and luxury, but always whilst looking for the best bargain. And he had to admit, he was pleased with the result. He'd found two, both leaving the day after the schools split up for spring break. Surely she couldn't find fault with either. He'd then contacted the cruise companies and had been able to negotiate a further discount on one and an upgrade with the other. So now, it was the moment of truth – would she like the one he'd chosen or should he have left it all to her?

Chapter Sixteen

'Morning, Paul. Nice jumper,' Amy said as she and Bella entered the school.

'Thank you,' Paul said, giving them a twirl and showing off his multicoloured jumper featuring a pug wearing Christmas tree sunglasses, a bandana covered in red reindeer, and with a red bell hanging from its collar. But that wasn't all. It had Santa figures covering its ears, and mini Santa hats, Christmas stockings, baubles, candles, candy canes and stars all over the cream background, which was also dotted with Christmas trees. In fact, it would be easier to say what his Christmas jumper was missing.

'I see the theme is subtle this year, Paul,' Bella said, grinning.

Paul laughed. 'That's right. I'm glad you got the memo.'

'What's a memo?' Bella teased him.

'Yeah, very funny. You've never heard of a fax either. You're not that young.'

'Hey! Cheeky! And we might have heard of faxes, but we've never used them,' Amy said.

'Anyway, have you ladies remembered your Christmas jumpers today?'

'What are you, the Christmas jumper police?' Amy

muttered, and Bella laughed.

'Yes, we have indeed.' Bella shrugged out of her coat to reveal she was wearing an elf outfit with bells at her wrists. 'I even have pointy shoes to change into,' she confided.

Paul frowned. 'That doesn't sound very comfortable.'

'Ah, Paul, we have to suffer for our art.' Amy removed her coat. 'Ta-da.' She was wearing a red Christmas jumper which read 'Oh What Fun' in glittery gold lettering inside a wreath of candy canes and Christmas stockings. Black leggings adorned with gingerbread men and candy canes completed her look.

'Well, ladies, I think it's fair to say we've embraced the spirit of the season.'

As the bell rang and Bella and Amy were about to put their coats back on to go fetch the children from the playground, Mr McCafferty walked out into the foyer, stopping Bella and Amy in their tracks.

He was wearing a green suit covered in Santas, candy canes, Christmas puddings, mistletoe, reindeer and snowmen. It even had a matching tie.

The headmaster grinned as he took in their gobsmacked expressions. 'What? Doesn't it suit me?'

Bella flushed and Amy stammered, 'It-it's certainly a look!'

'It's like you've stepped out of one of the Santa Clause movies,' Bella said.

Mr McCafferty beamed at them. 'Excellent. Right, shall we let the little darlings in from the cold then?'

Bella took a moment to compose herself; she was still so stunned at seeing the usually staid headmaster joining in with the Christmas theme. That said, one of the teachers had texted her, saying they'd seen him out jogging with

Paul at the weekend. But she hadn't believed that. Now she was wondering if it could be true.

She was looking forward to today – she loved seeing all the effort the children had gone to with their Christmas jumpers and outfits. Some of them went a little further and added deely boppers and other accessories.

Plus, the nativity was today and she and Amy had worked hard with the children to have everything as perfect as possible for the big day. It was a shame the choir competition was in only two days' time, as it would have been more relaxing to have the events spaced out a little, and to have more time to prepare … and recover. Steeling herself for a full-on but fun day, she threw open the doors to the playground.

The morning had been very busy with everyone chattering and the teachers directing everyone involved in the nativity to their places. Lara wasn't in the nativity this year. She'd been a wise man the year before, and since she had her solo in the choir competition in two days, she was glad. She had butterflies in her tummy whenever she thought about doing the solo. She was relaxed about the songs she'd sing with her friends, but although she'd practised the solo a million times, the thought of standing in front of all those people in the town square, with all the different schools and their families there, made her heart flutter and her mouth go dry. She hoped she didn't freeze up.

As she sat watching the nativity, she caught sight of the headmaster. Mr McCafferty's suit had been a big hit today. She smiled. He was smiling and singing along with the song, looking at those onstage and nodding to them in encouragement. Yes, things were going to plan where Mr McCafferty was concerned. She noticed her teacher, Mrs Hopkins, down the front of the hall, conducting the nativity from a chair set in the middle of the aisle. Mrs Dalwood was backstage, sending everyone on, she thought, at the right time. Certainly, that had been the case during the rehearsals. She frowned. She still had some work to do on Mrs Hopkins. The sadness in her eyes was still there most of the time. Lara knew she thought no one noticed as she tried to be happy and bright in class, but Lara had watched her when the children were all meant to be busy with their tasks, and her teacher's smile often slipped when she thought no one was looking.

Ivy came on just then and Lara giggled. Her bright yellow star costume was huge and inflatable and she looked enormous in it, with her skinny little arms and legs poking out of the sides and the bottom. She and Ivy had been rehearsing her lines for the past week at playtime. Ivy had been almost as nervous about being a star in the nativity as Lara was about possibly making a fool of herself in front of hundreds of people at the town square.

As Ivy delivered her lines, Lara was muttering them under her breath, willing her on. When her friend didn't stumble over any of them, and even added a joke of her own at the end, Lara's happiness levels soared and her Christmas spirit level replenished.

Lara noticed Ivy's parents sitting a couple of rows from the front. They both looked so happy watching Ivy onstage, but before the nativity started, and the parents were waiting for everyone to prepare, they hadn't been talking to each other; instead Mr Nicol had been texting and Mrs Nicol had been staring into space, her eyes widening occasionally as if she were trying to stay awake. Yes, Lara still had work to do there too.

This year's nativity was great, and Ivy was definitely the star of the show. The only moment when things didn't go quite to plan was when Toby, playing the part of myrrh, one of the wise men's gifts, slipped and knocked over the other two gifts, who then fell on top of each other and into the stable. Everyone had laughed, including those who had had to pick themselves up off the straw, and the adults in the audience had loved it, too, if their laughter was anything to go by.

Soon the nativity was over and it was time to return to class. In the hallway, Lara bumped into Ivy's mum and dad.

'Oh, hi, Lara. Did you enjoy the nativity?' Mrs Nicol asked.

'It was great, but Ivy was the star,' said Lara.

'Literally,' interrupted Mr Nicol.

'Well, good luck for your solo, Lara. I'd love to be there, but it's too noisy for the twins.'

'I know. Thanks.'

'I hope they're recording it. I'd love to hear it. I must ask your mum to video it.' Mrs Nicol patted her shoulder. 'You'll do great.'

Lara smiled and was just thinking how she could improve things between her friend's mum and dad when Mr Nicol raised his hand. 'High five, kiddo! Knock 'em dead.'

When Lara held up her hand and delivered the high five, Ivy's dad said, 'Wow, I got an electric shock off you there.'

Lara smiled and as she walked away, she thought, *That's what you think.*

Lara had a dental appointment that afternoon and was worried in case she had to have a filling done or an injection that made her tongue go floppy as she was afraid it would affect her singing, but her mum had insisted she had to go. Since her mum was picking her up a little earlier than school finished, Lara had to sit in the area next to the school office.

As she waited, a man came to the door and rang the bell to the office. Once he entered, Lara heard him ask Mrs Chalmers if Mrs Hopkins was in today. When she heard Mrs Chalmers call him Mr Hopkins, she smiled to herself. Another piece in the puzzle was about to be complete.

At the moment Mr Hopkins was about to be buzzed through to the waiting area, Lara launched herself off her seat and almost collided with him as she tripped on her way to speak to Mrs Chalmers. She went sprawling on the floor and everything in her school bag flew out of it. She lay there for a millisecond before Mr Hopkins said, 'Are you all right?'

Lara, pretending to be shaken, said, 'I think so.'

As she held her arm, Mr Hopkins gathered all her belongings and put them back in her bag. 'Here you go.'

'Thanks.' Lara smiled at him, and as he passed her bag to her, her hand brushed his. *Result.*

Mr Hopkins sat down, replacing Lara as her mum appeared at the front door to collect her. As the door closed behind her, Lara heard Mrs Chalmers say, 'Mr Hopkins, I'm sorry, but Mrs Hopkins has a meeting straight after class today. Will I tell her to call you?'

'No, it's OK, thanks. I'll catch up with her later.'

Chapter Seventeen

The following evening, Bella strolled along Main Street towards The Crooked Dug. She'd given in to Amy and decided to meet up with her and her husband, plus a few friends for a Christmas meal at their local pub. It was also quiz night, and although there were so many topics Bella knew nothing about, she thought she could hold her own on the quiz front. Plus, she didn't care if she didn't know many of the answers; it was the taking part and having fun that counted.

She sighed and her breath floated out in front of her. At least it wasn't raining.

At the town square, she stopped, shoved her hands deeper into her coat pockets and stared up at the fifty-foot-high Christmas tree. She'd missed the big switch-on this year as it had been parents' night. And quite frankly, she hadn't really been in the mood, what with Ryan leaving her. But tonight, whilst she stood looking up at the huge fir tree bedecked with gold and red ribbons and baubles to match, off-white lights twinkling like stars in the night sky, a flicker of hope surged through her. She *would* get through this. She was strong. She had friends, friends who were always there for her. Today, even the head had been happy, seemed like a different person even. If he could reinvent himself, so could she.

As for the nativity yesterday, it had, as usual, been wonderful, providing oodles of fun for the children, the staff and the parents. And nobody had been taken to A&E, which was a blessing.

Plus, the choir competition was tomorrow. The children were so excited about it. She was too. The whole school was. This year, they really had a chance, but she was conscious not to pile any pressure on Lara. She had a gut feeling that Lara performed best when in a more relaxed environment or when she wasn't in the spotlight. She did have reservations about how the day would go, but she prayed for Lara's sake that nerves didn't set in. She was such a good kid, and she deserved something wonderful at Christmas time. And the choir competition would be a positive experience for her.

'Hi.'

Bella froze at the sound of her husband's voice.

'What are you doing here?' he asked as she turned round to face him.

'I could ask you the same thing.' She took in the fine lines around his eyes. Maybe she wasn't the only one who was finding this hard. Her gaze dropped to his mouth and she involuntarily closed her eyes, the smell of his cologne infiltrating her nostrils. Sandalwood.

'I'm doing some last-minute Christmas shopping,' he said.

She opened her eyes and found him looking at her with an expression she couldn't quite read. Dismay? Regret?

When she didn't say anything, he said, 'Have you finished yours? You're usually nice and early.'

'Yep, all done, and wrapped,' she said, her tone not

inviting further conversation. She glanced at her watch. 'I'd best be going.'

'Somewhere to be?'

'Yes. I'm meeting…' Suddenly, she realised she didn't need to tell him. He was no longer a part of her life. She'd wanted him to be, but he'd chosen not to be. He'd ended their marriage. 'Anyway, have a nice Christmas.'

He stared at her, almost as if he couldn't believe she'd finished their conversation so abruptly. 'Yeah … you too.'

As Bella crossed the square and headed for The Crooked Dug, she didn't glance back. Not once. But it took all of her resolve not to do so.

'Elaine. Can you sit down a minute? I want to talk to you about something.'

'Let me just finish drying these dishes.'

'Elaine, please.'

Paul's wife turned to him and frowned, then the colour drained from her face. 'You're not ill, are you?'

'No, I'm not ill, but can you stop that and sit down? I've been trying to talk to you for the past few days, but something else has always come up – whether it's Christine phoning or Susan, or you've just got to nip out. I need to speak to you and it can't wait.'

'Right, what is it?' Elaine said, once she'd thrown the dishtowel down and slumped into the chair.

'Me retiring, or rather, me not retiring,' he said firmly.

He noted a sheepish look on Elaine's face, but he continued. He was determined to say his piece. 'Elaine, I know you don't like that I don't want to retire, but I love my job. I love the sense of purpose it gives me and I love the kids. I love the banter. At that school gate, I have a whole group of friends I talk to each day. Friends from all walks of life, all ages, with lots of different interests. It keeps me young.'

'Paul, I know–'

Paul held up a hand. 'Elaine, please just let me say this. I will retire, but when I'm ready. I'm not stopping you from doing any of your activities, and I will go and visit places with you and do more "stuff", but I wouldn't be happy if I retired next year, and I don't think *we* would be happy, as I'd be so unhappy I'd be a grumpy git. Do you understand?'

Elaine nodded. 'I do, Paul.' She put her hand on his arm. 'And I'm sorry. I've been really selfish and self-centred. I can't deny I do still find it difficult to accept that you don't want to retire, but at the end of the day, that's your decision. I shouldn't be trying to force you into something you don't want. I really am sorry.' She wrapped her arms around him and hugged him, as he kissed her on the top of her head.

'Thanks. I appreciate you saying that. There is just one more thing,' he said as he moved out of her embrace.

'Oh?' Elaine said.

'This.' He took an envelope from the pocket of his jacket, which was hanging over a nearby chair.

He hoped and prayed he'd got this right as he'd gone all-in in the end. He'd even asked Fraser's advice, something he wouldn't have done a week earlier.

Paul passed Elaine the envelope, which she turned over and over in her hands, like she was looking for some clue as to what all the mystery was about before opening it and withdrawing its contents.

As she read the letter then put her hand in and withdrew the remaining items, Paul waited for her to announce her verdict.

'Oh my God, Paul, have you booked this?' When he nodded, she said, 'Seventeen days in the Caribbean?'

He nodded again, and she went on, 'Saint Lucia, Saint Vincent, Antigua, Barbados…' Elaine jumped up and threw her arms around him. 'I love you, Paul Fairbairn. Oh my God! We're going to the Caribbean.' She stood up and danced around the room, like a child who has been told they can go to a concert of their favourite band despite the tickets being sold out.

Paul smiled. Thank goodness that plan worked out. Now he would count the seconds before the word 'shopping' was mentioned, as one thing was for sure – his wife would need a whole new wardrobe to go to the Caribbean.

'Over here, Bella!'

Bella spotted Amy's frantically waving hand and weaved her way through the pub towards their table. She nearly knocked into the pub's Christmas tree as someone who was a little the worse for wear backed into her, then apologised profusely as they sloshed beer all over her coat.

'Sorry! Merry Christmas, though,' said the culprit.

Sighing, Bella unbuttoned her coat and headed for a seat on the other side of Amy. Red, green and gold crackers sat beside each place setting and an enormous centrepiece with the word H O P E dominated the middle.

Amy leant in to give her a kiss, but noting her wet coat said, 'Ugh, what happened to you?' as she stepped back from her.

'Some idiot who's had a few too many knocked into me as I was coming in. Don't suppose you have any tissues, do you?'

'Here. I do,' said a voice.

Bella turned to see who had spoken. A pair of twinkling blue eyes met hers. Their owner was in the process of taking something out of his jacket pocket.

'Sorry. Bella, this is Matthew. He's Dylan's cousin.'

'Hi, Matthew. If you have some tissues that'd be great.'

She hung her coat on the coatrack behind them, and taking the tissues Matthew offered, dabbed it as best she could.

'Drink?' Matthew asked, materialising beside her.

'Sorry, what?' His proximity was unnerving her, and a twinge of something she couldn't quite name took root inside her.

'I'm getting a round in. Would you like a drink?'

Bella blew out a breath. 'Would I ever.' She hesitated. She'd been about to ask for a glass of Prosecco, but that was too expensive to ask a stranger to buy, even a kind, handsome stranger like this one. Well, they weren't strangers now – Bella had introduced them.

'Prosecco?' he asked.

How had he guessed? Her incredulity must have escaped into her expression as Matthew laughed and said, 'I'm not clairvoyant. Amy told me that's your usual.'

If she had a usual. That would suggest she went out regularly. She didn't.

'Prosecco would be lovely, thanks.'

He grinned and said, 'I'll be right back.'

She finished dabbing at her coat as 'Driving Home For

Christmas' belted out of the sound system.

'Bella, come and choose what you're having to eat. I'm starving and it's heaving in here tonight. I want to get our orders in well before the quiz starts, as I'd like time to eat the food whilst it's still warm.'

That seemed like a solid idea, and as Bella perused the menu, her stomach rumbled.

'Hungry, are we?' Matthew said as he placed her Prosecco in front of her.

'Just a bit.' Traitorous stomach. Great, and now she'd be drinking on an empty one. That was never advisable. 'Thanks for the drink.'

He dipped his head in acknowledgement, raised his wine glass and said, 'Cheers,' then clinked it with hers.

'Cheers!' Their eyes met for a moment before Bella looked away, hoping she didn't flush with embarrassment. She wouldn't even be able to blame it on the alcohol as this was her first drink. Anyway, liquid courage. She took a sip. It was divine. She clinked glasses with Amy as her friend introduced her to the others. Friends of her husband Dylan and Amy's friend from university.

Luckily, once they'd ordered, their food arrived quickly and Bella took no time in demolishing her root vegetable and almond tart, or her maple and cinnamon glazed pork belly. When talk of dessert started, she groaned. 'I'm stuffed. Can't we have a wee break before dessert? If not, I'll need to go for a nap.'

She really fancied the rhubarb and apple crumble, but right now she had no space.

'Oh, I'm sure that's not necessary. We're not that boring, are we?' Matthew pulled a face.

'The company's not at all boring this evening,' Bella

said, flirting just a little. Oh well, she'd be divorced soon enough and life was pretty crap at the moment. The least she could do was engage in a bit of friendly banter with her friend's husband's cousin at Christmas.

'Refill, Bella?' Amy said. 'My turn to get the drinks in, and I want to go now as I can see the quizmaster getting ready – he's already handing round pens and answer sheets.'

'Same again, then, please,' said Bella.

As her friend went to the bar, Matthew slipped in beside her. 'So, what are your quizzing strengths?'

Initially taken aback, as she hadn't seen him move from the other side of the table to hers, Bella said, 'Let me think. Science fiction movies and novels, geography, music from the twenty-first century?'

Matthew grinned. 'Well, we have the last part in common, at least, although I'm not bad on geography.'

'What are *your* strengths then?'

Matthew tilted his head to the side then said, 'Hmm, lacrosse, polo and backgammon moves.'

'Really?' He didn't look the type.

'No, I'm just messing with you. I only know polo involves horses and perhaps a pole or a net or something. Saw it in a movie.'

Bella laughed. 'Yes, I think that's the extent of my knowledge on it too. So, if that's not what you're good at, what are you good at?'

A smile danced upon Matthew's lips and Bella could almost see the speech bubble coming out of his head saying, '*Wouldn't you like to know?*', but she cleared her throat and averted her gaze for a second, picking up her Prosecco glass and taking a sip just as Matthew said, 'Ten-pin bowling, rugby and karaoke.'

Bella spluttered then choked and coughed. Matthew, concern crossing his face, said, 'You OK?'

She nodded but continued to cough. Matthew patted her back gently, but she had to gulp in air and take a moment before she regained her equilibrium.

'Thanks,' she said, eyes watering. She hoped her mascara wasn't running. Panda eyes was not a good look.

'I didn't realise my strengths would come as quite such a shock,' Matthew teased, eyes glinting with humour.

Bella gave him a weak smile. 'I didn't have you down for much of a karaoke singer.'

'Ah, so you've been thinking about me.'

Whilst she'd been enjoying the evening's light-hearted banter, Bella was now mortified. Matthew was lovely, fun, possibly clever – she'd find out during the quiz – and hot. But although she'd come out of her comfort zone – staying at home – she didn't feel ready for anything else.

'Question one.'

Silence fell over the bar for a moment.

'Yes, that got your attention. We're not quite ready to ask the questions yet. This is your five-minute warning. Get your drinks in, finish your dinner and be ready, as I will show no mercy, Christmas or not,' said the quizmaster. 'Don't put your hand up and say you missed the first five questions and can I repeat them, as you were at the bar, toilet, finishing your pudding. I will not be repeating any questions until the very end. Is that clear?'

'Yes, Santa.'

'Excellent. Ho ho ho, and Merry Christmas!'

Saved by the bell, Bella thought, then she nudged Amy's shoulder as she returned to the table. 'Will we order those desserts now?'

'Good plan. I'll grab the waiter.'

'I'll have the chocolate mousse.'

The quiz proved good fun, and when it finally paused for a break, Bella went up to order some more drinks as 'Do They Know It's Christmas?' belted out from behind the bar.

'Two glasses of Prosecco, two large glasses of Sauvignon Blanc, a pint of cider and three gin and tonics, please.'

As the barman prepared the drinks, Bella gazed around her. Christmas wreaths in red, green and snowy white covered the doors to the toilets, exits and kitchen, whilst drop fairy lights hung all around the bar, bathing it in a festive glow.

'I came to see if you wanted a hand,' a voice said close to her ear. She looked up to see Matthew standing over her. He must be just under six feet, Bella thought.

'Thanks. That would be great. I don't see any trays.'

'No, I think they've abandoned that idea for the night. Might be used as weapons.'

Bella laughed. 'It's not that bad in here, or rather, it's not usually that bad in here.'

'Exactly. Oh!'

Bella looked to see what had caught Matthew's attention and her heart both sank and raced at the same time. They were standing directly under the mistletoe.

'Well, how about it, Bella?' Matthew raised his eyes to the mistletoe before returning his gaze to her.

Suddenly, the evening's slightly flirty banter didn't seem like such a great idea. She wasn't ready. She was still married. She still wanted to be married.

'I-I-I–'

'I think you're in my place, mate,' a voice said.

Bella turned to see Ryan looking at her with such tenderness that it made her heart lurch. She vaguely recalled the barman saying, 'That's thirty-two sixty,' before Ryan touched his lips to hers and his arms slipped around her back, holding her against him.

'I'm sorry, Bella. For everything.' He paused then took a deep breath. 'I have something I need to tell you, but not here.' He looked around as Matthew, clearly summing up the situation and realising he was the third wheel, said, 'I'll leave you two to it.'

Bella shot him an apologetic glance over Ryan's shoulder and mouthed, 'Sorry.' Her eyes met Amy's, and Amy ushered her away with a wave of her hand.

As Bella and Ryan walked outside, he said, 'Can we head over to the square and talk? I'd prefer to be away from the noise of the pub so I can think straight. I came to the school yesterday and had everything planned out in my head, but it's gone now.'

Bella frowned. 'You came to the school?'

'Yes, but you had a late meeting, so I left.'

That gave Bella pause for a moment. She debated whether to dig her heels in and tell him he had to spit it out now, whatever it was, but then she decided it wouldn't hurt to hear him out, or to get another glimpse of the Christmas tree in the town square. Plus, it was Christmas, after all.

They walked to the square in relative silence, Bella wondering what was going through Ryan's head, and why he'd chosen now to accost her. She could be back in the warmth having fun with friends. This had better be good.

When they reached the tree, Ryan stopped and stared

up at it for a moment, then looked at Bella with such sorrow in his eyes that Bella's heart ached. What was going on? Was he ill? Had something happened? Fear clutched at her heart.

He sighed heavily then turned towards her, taking her hands in his and holding them tight as if he never wanted to let go.

Tears formed in his eyes and now she was truly worried.

'I'm sorry, Bella.'

Had he been unfaithful? Was that it?

'I've made such a mess of things. I went about this all wrong. I thought I was protecting you and all I've done is cause you so much pain.' He paused and tears ran down his face. He let go of her hand and swiped at them with the back of his hand.

'Protecting me? From what?' she couldn't help but ask.

'Bella, I love you. I always have, but I can't give you what you want, what you need.'

She frowned, confusion and uncertainty mingling in her mind. 'What do I want? What do I need?'

'Kids. I can't have children, Bella.'

'What?' She took one of his hands in hers. 'What do you mean?'

'I went to see the doctor as I was constantly exhausted. I was worried I had chronic fatigue syndrome or something. I didn't think it was normal for someone my age to be so drained all the time. I'm young, fit, virile.' He gave a bitter laugh. 'Or so I thought.'

When his eyes met Bella's, she thought she'd cry too. Her heart was simultaneously thumping and falling through the floor like a stone.

'The doctor suggested some blood tests to check my testosterone levels. I scoffed at him to start with – why would I need that checked? But then he outlined his reasons, and I agreed, not thinking for a second there was anything to be concerned about. Until the results came back. Then they did a sperm count. And it was low, so low the doctor asked me if I intended to have children, and told me that if I did, I should seek advice from a specialist.

'I saw the specialist. He ran some more tests and told me although it wasn't impossible for me to father children, it was highly unlikely and I'd be better reviewing other options.

'Bella, I know how much you want children – lots of them – I do, too, and I couldn't let you make that sacrifice. I know you'd have chosen me. I know you love me as much as I love you, but I couldn't put that on you. I couldn't take the possibility of being a mum away from you.'

As Bella took in the enormity of what Ryan was saying to her, her lip trembled and she knew tears weren't far away. She steeled herself and said, 'But, Ryan, we could have worked it out. We could adopt. We could…'

'Bella…'

So much was unsaid in that one word. He knew how much giving birth to a child of her own meant to her, carrying her own baby, being pregnant. They'd joked about it.

'Ryan.' She straightened up, holding herself tall. 'That wasn't your choice to make. At least, not yours alone.' She saw the pain mixed with love shining from his eyes and continued. 'You're right, I would have chosen you, in a heartbeat, but you didn't give me that chance, that choice. And you've been horrible to me, made me feel like nothing, like I didn't matter, and I couldn't work out why everything had gone so wrong.'

Tears spilled down her cheeks as Ryan stood before her, placing his hands on her upper arms.

'I know, and I'm so sorry. I've been so angry, not with you, but at the unfairness of it all. It was too much to cope with. I thought I could handle dealing with this knowledge and protect you, but instead I turned into someone I barely recognised.'

As his eyes met Bella's again, he said, 'I'm not asking you to take me back – I can't ask that – but I decided you should know the truth. That you needed to know the truth. I love you and I miss you more than I'll ever be able to explain.'

Bella looked into Ryan's eyes and wrapped her arms around him, burying her head in his chest. It was a lot to take in – his inability to have children and where they went from here, but she loved him, he was her husband, and she wasn't giving up on them so easily. Whilst his idea may have been a noble one, he'd gone about it all wrong. Once she digested this, she'd add her opinion and ideas, but for now, she just wanted to offer him reassurance, and equally needed it from him.

When she finally eased away from him, she said, 'Ryan, we've always had each other's backs, and as far as I'm concerned, that hasn't changed. I don't think we're going to resolve all of this under the Christmas tree, so why don't we go home and try to talk this out?'

The relief on Ryan's face made Bella want to weep. Her poor husband, despite how awful he'd made her feel, had been carrying this secret around for months. Right then, she knew, whatever it took, however hard this was, she would support him and they would find a way.

That night they didn't make love – she wasn't ready for that – but after talking downstairs for hours, they lay in bed, wrapped around each other like a figure eight.

Whilst she hadn't totally forgiven him yet for everything he'd put her through, she now had hope they would make it, after all, and their marriage could be repaired. Ryan had confessed he'd been so stricken by the news, he hadn't known what to do, and in true ostrich fashion, had initially shoved his head in the sand until events had led to him exploding and declaring he was moving out, and then that he wanted a divorce. Fear of failure and of messing up her life and taking from her the one thing he knew she wanted above all else had been the root of those knee-jerk decisions.

Before he'd left for work the next morning, he'd asked if it was OK to move back in. With the knowledge of what he'd been about to give up for her, to protect her, she'd thrown her arms around him and said yes.

Chapter Eighteen

The crowds had come out in force for the singing competition of the year. By some miracle, Christmas or otherwise, the sun was shining and it wasn't as cold as it had been in recent days. Although the children were all wrapped up, there had been some concerns about how the elderly who liked to come and watch would cope if the weather was bad, but today it seemed like the gods were shining down on them. Whatever the reason, Bella was elated.

'Miss, I'm not sure I can do it.' Lara stood to Bella's side, looking up at her earnestly.

Bella took a gentle hold of Lara's upper arms. 'Lara, I have never heard anyone sing so beautifully as you. Even on your worst day of singing you would do better than most people. I won't force you to go on, you know that. But I'd love you to see everyone's reaction when you start to sing. They're all going to have goose bumps.'

Lara searched Bella's eyes. 'Really?'

Bella nodded. 'Really. Isn't that right, Mrs Dalwood?'

Amy turned. 'What was that?'

'I was just saying everyone's going to have goose bumps when Lara sings her solo.'

'Lara, not only will they have goose bumps, their goose

bumps will have goose bumps!'

Lara grinned and Amy patted her arm and said, 'Lara, you have an amazing voice. Let it loose and let everyone hear it. OK?'

Lara looked into Amy's eyes and then nodded. 'OK.'

When the choirs from all the schools began to sing 'Away in a Manger', a hush fell over the crowd, who had until then been chatting animatedly. As each successive school sang individually, the cheers went up and the judges furiously marked their scorecards. *Please let us win this year. We deserve it. The kids deserve it.*

As Heatherwood took to the miniature stage, Bella stamped her feet to try to stay warm and gave the children the thumbs-up sign. She stood with Amy, Fraser, who had joined them moments earlier, and Paul, who arrived with Tabitha, Jacob and Sophie right before Heatherwood was due to go on.

'Sorry I'm late, we got stuck in traffic,' said Tabitha.

Bella smiled at them, but she also noticed the headmaster give Tabitha a warm smile too. Interesting.

Fraser wrapped his scarf more tightly around his neck as all the choirs grouped together again and sang '*Adeste Fideles*' and the soloists from each school stepped up. He noted the children huddling together and hoped they weren't freezing. He wasn't toasty, but then some of them wore those padded ankle-length coats that he was beginning to wish were in vogue for men too.

He'd honestly thought Heatherwood and maybe Ferntree were the two schools to watch. Now as the soloists began, the hairs on his arms pricked up. St Peter's Primary's soloist would give the chap who sang *The Snowman* a run for his money. His rendition of 'The First Noel' took his breath away. A few others still had to sing before it was Lara's turn. He'd heard her practising, and every time she sang, his heart lifted. There was an innocence, a hopefulness, a joyousness in her singing that made *him* have hope and feel joyful.

The next few children were good, but not exceptional, not like the boy from St Peter's. Maybe he had the top apostle helping him. Fraser chuckled at his own inner joke.

When the boy from Ferntree sang 'Mary, Did You Know?', Fraser thought there was a good chance Ferntree would take the double, and he exchanged a worried look with Mrs Hopkins. As Lara's solo came closer, Fraser edged towards Tabitha.

'She'll be amazing,' he said. 'I've been listening to her from my office, which is next to the games hall, as you know. Her singing is incredible.'

Tabitha smiled. 'I know, but *she* needs to believe that.'

'Well, I can tell you, she has certainly had plenty encouragement from Mrs Hopkins, and Mrs Dalwood.'

'Yeah, they've been fantastic with her.'

A shiver ran through Tabitha and she visibly trembled. 'Brr. Why can't this happen in the summer?' she joked.

'Here. Take my scarf,' said Fraser, unwinding it and passing it to her. He'd thought of wrapping it around her neck and pulling her towards him… 'Oh, here she is. Lara's up next.'

The quiet murmur that had run through the crowd between choirs and then between soloists ceased immediately Lara began to sing.

'O Holy Night! The stars are brightly shining…'

As she sang, Fraser felt his throat start to close up with the effort of not showing emotion. It was so hauntingly beautiful. He'd never been affected to this extent by music before. Sniffing, he turned to see Tabitha had tears rolling down her face. Her brother and Sophie were oblivious, their attention on Lara. Fraser patted his pockets, but didn't have any tissues with him. Beside him, Mrs Hopkins nudged him, her eyes bright, and passed him some tissues, which he gave to Tabitha. Close by, he spotted Paul, who had removed his glasses to wipe his eyes. It seemed Lara had the same effect on all of them.

Lara's voice rose to a crescendo and Fraser's mouth split into a broad smile. Tabitha's face was shining with pride at her daughter, and rightly so. When Lara sang the last note and stepped back from the microphone, her radiant smile was wonderful to see. She deserved this accolade. Everyone cheered far louder and for far longer than they had for anyone else, and Fraser noted the crowd had swelled since the previous soloist as people doing their shopping or going about their day stopped to listen.

When Lara left the stage, she made a beeline for Tabitha. 'Mum, I did it!'

'You did, sweetheart, and you were incredible.' Tabitha covered Lara's head in kisses and hugged her to her.

As her uncle and aunt were congratulating Lara, Mrs Hopkins came forward. 'Lara, that was amazing.' Her eyes were shining with unshed tears. 'It was so moving. I'm so proud of you.'

'Thank you, Mrs Hopkins.'

Ivy made her way through the crowd and flung her arms around Lara's neck. 'Lara, that was brilliant. You were the best by miles. Wasn't she?' Ivy eyed everyone as if daring them to disagree.

A murmur of 'I thought so' went up around them.

'They kept the best for last,' said Paul, smiling at Lara.

There was a fifteen-minute waiting period whilst the judges made their final decision. Hot drinks stalls had been positioned at two ends of the square and helpers were distributing tea, coffee and hot chocolate to those present.

'This waiting is killing me,' said Tabitha.

'Me too,' agreed Mrs Hopkins.

'How do you think I feel?' said Ivy. 'She's my best friend.'

They all laughed and Fraser said, 'How are you feeling, Lara?'

'Nervous, but glad it's over.'

'Did you enjoy it, though?' asked Mrs Hopkins, wrapping an arm around her.

'I loved it,' said Lara, her eyes shining. 'I wish I could do it all again.'

A hush finally fell as one of the judges picked up a microphone and stood up. 'Thank you everyone for coming to this year's A Carol for Christmas. I'm sure you'll all agree the entries have been absolutely phenomenal. And I hope you've all enjoyed the incredible performances. It has been exceptionally difficult to judge both the group category and the soloist category this year. However, that's what we're here for, and we have made our decision.

'In the choir competition, third place goes to Ferntree Primary.'

Shouts and cheers went up as Ferntree returned to the makeshift stage to collect their trophy.

Once the noise had settled down and Ferntree had cleared the stage, the judge announced the runner-up. 'In second place is Heatherwood Primary. Well done!'

The whole choir flew up onto the stage, Ivy and Lara rejoining them, amid cheers from the teaching staff and parents. Ivy lifted the plaque aloft and everyone cheered.

'And in first place is St Peter's Primary. Congratulations.'

St Peter's collected the crystal star-shaped trophy and Fraser smiled when he saw their headteacher take it from the boy who had been holding it. He clearly didn't want it being dropped and broken.

After the furore had died down, the judge said, 'I will now pass you to one of my fellow judges for the soloist competition winners.'

One of the male judges rose from his seat at the judging table and replaced his female counterpart. He said a few words about how honoured he was to judge the competition and Fraser wished he would hurry up and put them all out of their misery.

'In third place, from St Ronan's Primary, Agata Simpson.'

Whistling and cheering ensued and Agata, a tiny girl with blonde wavy hair halfway down her back, smiled and shook the judge's hand.

'In second place, from Ferntree Primary, Mikey Rostock.'

Tabitha and Fraser looked at each other. He wanted to hold her hand in reassurance but knew he couldn't. He did the next best thing; he smiled and crossed his fingers in front of her and then his legs, making her laugh.

'In first place, with an absolutely outstanding rendition of "O Holy Night", Lara Field.'

But the party from Heatherwood hadn't even waited to

hear Lara's name before they began cheering and celebrating. As soon as they heard 'O Holy Night', they knew, and there was cheering and whooping and hollering and calling of Lara's name.

Fraser turned to Tabitha, and with great restraint he stopped himself from leaning in to kiss her gently on the lips, but he also saw a flicker of something in Tabitha's eyes that gave him hope.

Lara reached the podium only for the judge to say, 'Well done, Lara. Your performance was emotional, strong and we loved it. Congratulations.' He passed the trophy to her – a brass songbird – and Lara shyly held it against her and said, 'Thank you.'

Someone in the crowd shouted, 'Hold it up so we can see it!'

So she held it up high and the crowd clapped and cheered, until the judge spoke into the microphone.

'Congratulations to young Lara. Now that wraps up this year's A Carol for Christmas competition. There's only one more thing.' He turned to Lara. 'Lara, would you mind singing your carol for us one more time?'

Lara beamed with pleasure and nodded, then he passed her the microphone, and once everyone had settled down again, Lara began to sing.

'I wish I hadn't given those tissues away now,' Mrs Hopkins whispered as tears ran down her face and she wiped under her eyes with her fingers.

As Lara's voice floated out into the crowd, Fraser thought there may be hope for Christmas this year after all.

Chapter Nineteen

'I can't believe you've talked me into this, Jacob,' said Fraser. 'It's freezing.'

Jacob laughed. 'You'll be fine when you warm up a bit. Once you're running, you don't even really feel it.'

'Why don't I believe that?' Fraser turned to Paul, who shrugged.

'I can't argue with what Jacob said, but then I'm used to running in the freezing cold.'

'You're just cocky because you've been beating me in our practices.'

Paul raised both arms out to his sides. 'If you've got it, it's a shame not to flaunt it.'

'When are you retiring again?' Fraser said.

'Ha! Not soon enough for you.' He glanced behind him. 'And don't say that in earshot of Elaine and give her ideas again. She'll have me playing bowls and golf if you mention retirement in her presence.'

Jacob said, 'Didn't she want you to go on lots of cruises?'

Paul nodded. 'Yeah, but I think the money would run out quite quickly at the rate she was talking about. Back to back or once every couple of months or something. She seems to have forgotten to tell me about her lottery win.'

but it wasn't the same, and everyone knew flights were cancelled all the time in the US at this time of year. All you had to do was watch the latest Hallmark Christmas movie, or listen to the news.

Ivy chattered all the way home, her excitement almost tangible. It saddened Valerie that Munro wouldn't see her joy when she found the Christmas Eve box Santa had left her, or when her elf wrote her a message telling her to be good and how he'd really enjoyed spending time with her this year. And even though the twins were too young to do much yet, apart from gurgle and need feeding and changing, he risked potentially missing their first Christmas. Plus, he was leaving her to do everything all on her own. Their nine-year-old daughter shouldn't have to be a surrogate parent in her father's absence.

Valerie didn't think she could even give him the gourmet food and drink hamper she'd ordered months ago for him, as she was so upset.

As she pulled into the driveway, the strains of 'Fairytale of New York' reached her ears. It was her favourite Christmas song. She opened the door to the most unbelievable aroma. What was that? Smelled like bacon, but what else? Was that roast chestnuts? Had her in-laws come to visit? Oh no, she hated guests arriving unannounced, especially when she'd been out all day and hadn't had a chance to tidy up or prepare, but as she walked into the living room, shedding her coat as she went, she saw Munro sitting on the sofa, a bottle in each hand, feeding the twins, as they lay on cushions on either side of him.

'What the–?'

'Hi.' Munro beamed at her. 'How was the shopkeeping

experience?'

'It was good.' She eyed Munro nervously. 'Who's cooking?'

'I am.' He gestured to the twins. 'They just needed feeding, but it's all under control.'

'And what are we having? It smells really good, by the way.'

'Glazed ham with orange sauce, chestnuts and green beans almondine.'

Valerie raised an eyebrow. 'What was the last thing?'

'Green beans almondine. Basically, sautéed green beans with toasted almonds.'

Valerie felt her other eyebrow raise. 'Who are you and what have you done with my husband?'

Munro laughed. 'I thought you could do with some haute cuisine after a hard shift in the café.'

'True, although I think Ivy may go into a sugar coma. I'm sure she and Lara were overindulging in the hot chocolate and cupcake department.'

Munro smiled, and for a moment it felt like the old easy way things used to be with them, before his job had superseded all else.

'Do you have enough time to eat it before you head to the airport, though?'

'Ah, about that.' Munro shifted as the bottle fell from Noah's mouth, his little features perfect as he drifted off to sleep. Poppy, the slightly larger twin, was still sucking away contentedly.

Valerie sat down on the sofa and kissed Noah's head then took him from Munro's grasp and popped him in the pram that stood behind the sofa. Meanwhile, Ivy sat down on the other side of Munro and let Poppy, who had noticed her big sister, grip her fingers.

'Yes?' Valerie said.

'I've postponed it.'

Valerie's heart leapt. Was he really putting them before the company?

'Really?'

'Really. And I'm sorry. I should never have considered it.' He took her hand in his and caressed the back of it. 'The meeting will be in the New Year now.'

Valerie looked at Munro, then said to Ivy, 'Sweetie, can you go get me some nappies from the upstairs bathroom, please?'

Ivy let go of Poppy's hand. 'Sure.'

As her elder daughter skipped off in search of nappies, Valerie said, 'What changed your mind?'

This time, Munro gripped both her hands in his. 'You. Them.' His look encompassed the three children, as he nodded his head towards the stairs to take in Ivy too.

'I remembered why I work the hours I do. It's not because I have any pressing desire to climb any ladders. Not any more. I do it for my family, and if I can't make sacrifices for my family, who can I make them for? In fact, I shouldn't even be calling it a sacrifice – it's my choice. I want to be here.'

For the first time in months, Valerie relaxed. Finally, she was hearing from her husband everything she'd wanted to hear. No, needed to hear.

'And I'm sorry I've taken you for granted, too. When you stormed out that day, it was a wake-up call. It is damn difficult to look after these two little 'uns. Much harder than I ever thought. But today, I really enjoyed it.'

'I'm sorry too,' said Valerie. 'I've been such a moany

cow, but I'm utterly exhausted all the time.'

'I know.' Munro squeezed her hand. 'And I'm going to help a lot more, I promise.'

As Ivy arrived back in the room with the nappies, Munro said, 'Damn it. I'd better check on dinner or it will be burnt to a crisp.' He stood up with Poppy, and Ivy said, 'Can I hold her, Dad? I like holding her when she's asleep. She's so perfect. Like a little doll.'

Munro gazed down upon Ivy and said, 'Just like her big sister.' He kissed Ivy on the head, hugged her to him, then said, 'Sit down, then, and I'll put her in your arms. Remember to cradle her head.'

Ivy looked at him and rolled her eyes. 'I know, Dad. This isn't my first rodeo, you know.'

Munro glanced at Valerie, who was creasing up. He passed Poppy to Ivy, then whispered in Valerie's ear, 'Where does she hear this stuff?'

'Your guess is as good as mine,' said Valerie as he leant over and kissed her on the lips.

The Nicol family would be together after all for the twins' first Christmas.

'I'd really like to–' began Munro.

'I know, but there's a glazed ham–'

'Damn it, I forgot – again.'

Valerie chuckled as Munro hared it to the kitchen. She could get used to this.

Chapter Twenty

'Mum, it's only one more sleep,' said Lara, as she hugged her from behind. Her mum was sitting in her pyjamas, cross-legged on the floor, wrapping a present, a cup of coffee on the table in front of her, as Lara plopped herself down beside her.

'Who's that for?'

'A friend.'

'Not for me then?' Lara's mouth turned down slightly at the corners.

'No, not for you. You have to wait for Santa to bring your presents.'

'Aw, but it's a whole other day.' Lara pouted. 'Why does it take so long?'

Tabitha smoothed Lara's hair with her fingers and cradled her against her shoulder. 'It's only twenty-four hours, and we have *Jolabokaflod* to look forward to today.'

Lara perked up. 'I have the best book to give Ivy. She's going to love it.'

'What is it? Did you use your pocket money to buy it?' her mum asked.

'Yep. It's *Pippi Longstocking*. Can you believe she hasn't read it already?'

'Remember, Lara, your aunt and uncle own a café next

to a bookshop, and you're there practically every day. Not everyone has that opportunity.'

'True, but Ivy is there a lot too.'

'Yes, but it's not quite the same thing. Anyway, great choice. She will love it.'

'I know.' Lara was feeling a little smug as she knew her friend so well, and couldn't wait to see her face. She wondered what book Ivy had chosen for her.

'Right, will we get ready? You and I could have our own little *Jolabokaflod* before everyone arrives.'

'That's a great idea, Mum. I'll be ready in five minutes.'

'It may take me a little longer, but we'll leave as soon as we can.'

'Morning, Uncle Jacob, Aunt Sophie,' said Lara when she and her mum arrived at Sugar and Spice.

'Morning, Squirt,' her uncle replied. 'You want to help me make some cakes before we open?'

'Sure, but is it OK if Mum and I explore the reading area first? We wanted to read together before it gets busy.'

'Of course. Hot chocolate coming right up.'

When Lara tilted her head, her uncle said, 'All part of the *Jolabokaflod* service.'

Lara gave him a double thumbs-up and headed over to the special reading area.

'It's so cosy, Mum. Here, take a blanket.' Lara shrugged off her winter coat and placed it on the coat stand, then threw the other end of the wool blanket to her mum.

Once her mum had removed her coat, too, they unzipped their boots, took them off, then snuggled under the blanket and tucked their feet in.

'Oh, Mum, this is the best way to start the day.'

Her mum's face shone with happiness as her uncle handed them both their hot chocolate, Lara's filled with marshmallows and whipped cream.

'You know you're my favourite uncle, don't you?' said Lara.

Her uncle rolled his eyes. 'Lara, I'm your only uncle.'

'Yeah. That's true–' she smiled sweetly '–but even if you weren't, you'd still be my favourite.'

Her uncle looked at his sister. 'Tabitha, I can't think where she gets her sass from.'

'Don't look at me,' Lara's mum said.

'Ha! You're like two peas in a pod. Right, some of us have work to do.'

'So, who's all coming here tomorrow for Christmas lunch?' her mum asked.

'Well, Stanley's coming. I'll go pick him up, and Tom and Jerry said they'd gladly come and make a donation to charity rather than cook.' He then rhymed off a few more and her mum sat back, sipping her hot chocolate but saying nothing.

'And are we all organised? Do you need me to do anything?'

Her uncle thought for a moment then said, 'At the moment, I think we have everything under control, but I'll let you know if I need anything at the last minute.'

'OK. Anyway, did you get Sophie a book?'

'Yes, several, actually, but I'll only give her one today.'

'Good, I'll take over at some point so you and she can settle down to enjoy *Jolabokaflod*.'

Her uncle rested his hand on her mum's shoulder and said, 'I'd appreciate that, sis.'

'Are you ready, Lara?' her mum said. 'I have a book to exchange with you.'

'You do? But I thought the book you were wrapping wasn't for me?'

Her mum smiled. 'It wasn't, but this one is.' She pulled a book from her bag. It was wrapped in navy blue paper topped with a gold ribbon.

'Ooh.' Lara held out her hands, then let them fall. 'I didn't get you anything.'

'But I did,' said her uncle, materialising beside them again, with a gold-coloured rectangular package.

'Thanks, Jacob,' her mum said.

'Don't mention it. Now, open up, then drink up, or that hot chocolate will be cold chocolate.'

Her mum shook her head at him. 'OK, bossy.' She rolled her eyes at Lara, who giggled.

Lara tore open her parcel to discover a copy of *Amari and the Night Brothers*, a book she'd been wanting for ages. She set the packaging to the side and said, 'Thanks, Mum.'

'You're welcome, sweetheart.'

'Open yours,' she said, and her mum undid the packaging and withdrew the book from within.

'*Precious*. Oh, thank you, Jacob.'

'Well, I know you like to add to your collection of jewel-themed books, so I figured this might fit the bill. Or rather, Tom did.'

Her mum smiled. 'He does give the best recommendations.'

'He really does. Right, I'll leave you two to it. Enjoy.'

'Come on, *Squirt*, let's snuggle down before everyone else arrives and we have to fight them for the blankets!'

Lara drained her hot chocolate, even the sticky wet

marshmallows at the bottom, wiped her mouth and hands on a napkin so as not to get any hot chocolate on her new book, and pulled the blanket over her.

She read the first two chapters out loud, then said, 'I think I'll read to myself now, so you can read your book.'

'Good idea, hon. This is lovely and cosy. I could stay here forever.'

'Me too,' said Lara, and she snuggled in closer and rested her head on her mum's shoulder as she turned to the third chapter.

Paul had mentioned the reading event to Elaine and she'd quite fancied it, so after a tidy-up of the house, they headed into town.

As they drove in, Paul told her of the tradition. 'So, people usually give gifts of books to their family or friends and then they sit together and read, in silence, or they discuss what they're reading. It's meant to be relaxing, they spend quality time together and get away from all the hectic activities of daily life.'

'We could certainly be doing with that,' said Elaine. 'Look at this traffic.'

Paul couldn't help but agree. It was busier in the town than the last few times he'd been to Sugar and Spice, but he supposed that was to be expected. People would be getting last-minute gifts, picking turkeys up from the butcher's and the various supermarkets, as well as meeting with friends and family.

They were relatively early; it was only nine thirty. Although it was already busy, there were a few seats left in the 'chilled reading area', whilst the café itself was full, most likely with shoppers about to brave the crowds.

'Oh no, I don't have a book to give you,' said Elaine, her hand flying to her mouth.

'Don't worry,' said Jacob, who had overheard. 'We have discount cards at the till for you to use next door in T&J's. They'll sort you out.'

As Elaine scuttled off to buy Paul a book, he sat back and relaxed and covered his legs with one of the blankets.

'Hey, Mr Fairbairn,' said Lara, who was curled up on the sofa opposite.

'Hi, Lara. Have you been here long?'

'Since before it opened. I love Jola … day.'

Paul laughed. 'Yes, I find it hard to say as well. I like Jola day better.'

She untucked herself from her blanket and came over to him, her book in her hand. 'Did you get Mrs Fairbairn a book? It's the rule, you know.'

'Don't you worry. I got her a book, and she is away to buy me one now. What's your book about?' He indicated to her hand.

'Oh, this, it's about a girl called Amari whose brother goes missing.'

Paul frowned. 'That seems a bit serious for Christmas Eve.'

'Ah, but there's magic in it. It's a fantasy book.'

'I see,' said Paul as the doorbell dinged and Fraser walked in. 'There's the headmaster.'

'School's out for the holidays.' Lara winked at him and retreated under her blanket again.

Fraser tipped his head to Paul, then spoke briefly to Jacob and Sophie. Paul saw Fraser pull a face before he pointed to a cake and placed his order.

'Hi, Paul, how are you? OK if I sit here?'

'Would you mind sitting this side of me? My wife's got dibs on that one.'

At Fraser's puzzled expression, he clarified. 'She's away into T&J's to get me a book.'

'Right,' said Fraser as the bell dinged again and Elaine walked in.

'There we go. Did you order the drinks? Oh, hi, Mr McCafferty.'

'Please call me Fraser. Hi, Mrs Fairbairn.'

'Elaine, please. So, Fraser, are you here on your own?'

Paul groaned inwardly. He loved his wife but she was every shade of everything except subtle.

'I am, but when I have all of you around me, I don't feel as if I'm on my own.' Fraser smiled brightly, but his discomfort shone from him as if an aura were surrounding him. 'Excuse me a second.'

As Fraser stood, the door to the kitchen opened and Tabitha walked out.

'Fraser, so glad you could make it.'

'Me too.' Fraser felt his face redden. 'I was going to grab a drink and something to eat then get myself a book from next door and join in the fun.'

'Good plan. Lara and I had a bit of a relaxation session here this morning, but now, as you can see–' she gestured to the tray of cakes in her hands '–I'm up to my eyes in it. Good thing we did it this morning.'

'Well, I'm glad you both got to spend a little bit of time embracing *Jo-la-bo-ka-flod* this morning.' He pronounced every syllable slowly, trying not to make a mess of it.

'Me too.' Tabitha stopped as if unsure what to say next.

Fraser found himself equally tongue-tied, but eventually said, 'Actually, perhaps later, when you've closed up, and maybe even when Lara has gone to bed, you might find time to read this.' He took a green and gold gift-wrapped parcel with an ice-white bow from his inside pocket. 'This is for you.'

'Oh, Fraser, thank you.' Tabitha set the tray of cakes on the counter and took the parcel he handed to her, rotating the gift for a moment before her eyes met his again. 'Can I open it now?'

He smiled widely. 'Please do.'

She undid the bow and opened the gift, exclaiming, 'Oh, I love it, Thank you.' She leant forward and kissed him on the cheek and Fraser inhaled sharply.

'*The Night Circus* has been on my ever-growing to-read list for ages.'

Fraser flushed and Tabitha said, 'Can you hold this one second?'

His brow creased as she pushed the book into his hands. 'Wait here.' She held up a finger. 'I'll be right back.' Then she barrelled back through the door to the kitchen.

He felt a bit of a lemon as he stood there, but she returned less than thirty seconds later and brandished a package at him. A similarly shaped package to the one he'd given her. No. Dare he hope she too had thought of him and chosen a book for him?

'Here. This is for you.' As Tabitha handed him the parcel, she said, 'When Jacob told me he'd mentioned the *Jolabokaflod* to you, I knew I wanted to buy you a book.'

Fraser gaped at her, but she rushed on. 'Now, I know it's not a thriller, and I might not have chosen the right type of book, but I think this book works for readers of many different genres.'

He stared at her, and her eyes twinkled at him. 'Go on then. Open it.'

With clumsy fingers, he undid the ribbon and took out *The Art of Racing in the Rain*. He didn't know it, hadn't heard of the author, so he glanced at Tabitha, and she said, 'Read the blurb.'

As he did, his lips curved up at the edges. The story was told from the point of view of a dog.

'It's not a new book,' Tabitha said, 'but it's one of my favourites.'

Fraser looked at Tabitha. 'Thank you. I can't wait to read it.' He looked round at the reading area, the sofas covered with blankets, where a couple was standing up to leave. 'Care to join me for ten minutes?'

'I-I-' She glanced at Jacob, who was standing at the counter. He grinned and ushered her away, giving her a none-too-discreet thumbs-up.

Fraser hid a smile, then gestured for Tabitha to sit on the sofa, as he sat himself opposite her.

'Mum?' Lara said.

Jacob swiftly cut in, 'Lara, I need a taste tester for the new cupcake frosting. Wanna help?'

As Lara leapt off her sofa and scrambled over to Jacob, Fraser mouthed 'Thank you' at him.

Paul had been observing what had occurred between Fraser and Tabitha. Elaine had been chatting to him, but he'd only managed to take in a fraction of what she'd said. He was glad for Fraser. It had saddened him the man was spending Christmas alone. It had crossed his mind to invite Fraser over to spend the day with him and Elaine, but much as he loved his wife, she was best appreciated in small doses.

'So, Elaine, here's your book.'

'Ooh, thanks. And here's yours.' They exchanged books, and soon Elaine was exclaiming over the creative non-fiction book he'd bought her about the Caribbean, whilst he sank further down in the blankets, sipped his hot chocolate and delved into the military thriller she'd bought him. You couldn't go wrong with a good thriller.

His head popped up when the doorbell pinged again and he spotted Ivy racing towards Lara, who had spent an inordinate amount of time taste-testing. Ivy withdrew a book from her backpack and Lara pulled her across to the sofa she'd bagsied earlier, then took a book out of her bag and gave it to her. They both opened their parcels at the same time and the joy on their faces, and the enthusiasm they showed for reading, was lovely to see. This was a great tradition, Paul thought. He glanced at Elaine. And if it kept his wife from babbling on so much, even better. He returned to his thriller and was soon engrossed in it, pulled out of the story only a good while later when Elaine asked if he wanted another drink.

When Valerie entered the café seconds after her daughter, she spotted Tabitha sitting on one of the sofas in the *Jolabokaflod* section, quietly reading, Fraser beside her. It was about time her friend was lucky in love, she thought. It had been far too long, and the only good thing that had come of Tabitha's relationship with Lara's father had been

Lara herself. She went up to the counter and said to Jacob, 'Hi, would you mind if I left Ivy here for a bit to read with Lara? I don't want to interrupt.' She inclined her head to where Fraser and Tabitha had their backs to her.

'Oh, absolutely no problem, but do come back later and try one of these.' He held up a cake and said, '*Sernik*, from Poland. Made it last night.'

It looked delicious. Some sort of cheesecake. 'What's in it?' she asked.

'*Twaróg*. It's a Polish cheese, and vanilla.'

'Jacob, I'll be back, don't you worry. I may leave my daughter, but I won't be leaving that cake. Please keep me two slices, one for me and maybe the other for Munro, or else just two slices for me.' She snickered and Jacob laughed as she gave him a wave and left to go for a walk around the town.

Valerie walked towards Winstanton's main square where the choir concert had taken place only a few days before. She'd been gutted to miss it, but she also knew standing out in the cold with two newborns wouldn't have been a wise decision. But when Ivy had been called in as a substitute because a child had gone down with a chest infection the night before, she'd been doubly upset to miss it. The sound of carollers came from nearby and as she reached the square she saw a small brass band performing in accompaniment. The strains of 'Silent Night' grew louder, and as she stood, listening to the music, gloved hands in her pockets to keep out the cold, she closed her eyes and lived in the moment.

She was able to simply be – feel, not think. As the carol continued, something landed on her eyelid, then once again, and she opened her eyes to witness large flakes of snow falling onto the stage and her clothes and the path she was standing on. She looked up and saw from the colour of the sky that they may well be in for a white Christmas. Tilting her face upwards, she let the flakes land on her, enjoying the coldness of them against her skin, then she opened her mouth and stuck out her tongue. She didn't know when she'd last thought to do this, if ever, but now seemed a good time. As the flakes fell faster, Valerie made a decision, and then a Christmas wish. When the flakes became a flurry, Valerie sighed with contentment, took one long, last, lingering look at the Christmas tree, then headed back to Sugar and Spice.

This Christmas promised to contain everything she ever wanted.

'I need to go. I have to head up to Bay Park to see Mum,' said Fraser. 'Thank you for the book and ... for our time together today.'

'Thank you, too. Today has been lovely.' Tabitha reached up and touched his cheek. Fraser enjoyed the sensation of her hand on his skin, then he clasped his hand over hers.

'This meant a lot to me today. Christmas is going to be ... different this year.'

'Oh, I know. That's a good thing, though, isn't it?'

Fraser frowned. He didn't really consider sitting at home on his own as a good thing. He was used to being in company at Christmas.

'Anyway, Merry Christmas. I hope you, Lara, Sophie and Jacob have a really good time.'

Tabitha glanced at him, her brow furrowing. 'But we'll

see you tomorrow, right?'

Fraser almost took a step back. 'Tomorrow?'

Tabitha smiled. 'Yeah, Christmas Day. Friends and family together. We'll be here, of course, with those who are important to us and a few people who don't have any loved ones close by, or those who want to make a donation to charity and come here for a slap-up meal.'

Fraser's brow creased in astonishment. 'Do you and Jacob ever take a day off?'

'Not if we can help it. So, tomorrow?'

'I'd love to, but I need to go visit Mum.'

Now Tabitha's face scrunched up in confusion. 'But your mum's coming here, with Stanley. Didn't she tell you?'

Fraser's mouth dropped open. 'She's what?' Then after a pause, he said, 'No, she didn't.'

'Stanley has been coming here for years, and this year he asked if your mum could come. We said yes. She said yes, but only on condition you could come, too, and of course I said yes to that. They're both coming here, and now, if you want to, so are you.'

'I-I, Tabitha, I don't want to take up someone's place, someone who's more deserving than me.'

'Fraser, I want you there, and not as someone who doesn't have somewhere to go. I want you there as a friend, my friend.'

Fraser's eyes searched hers. Was there some hope for them? He liked her, a lot. But there were complications.

'Then I'd be delighted to come. Thank you. Enjoy Christmas Eve with Lara. I'll see you tomorrow.' He kissed her cheek and she murmured, 'I'll text you the details.'

As Fraser opened the door to Sugar and Spice and a

wave of cold air blasted him, he thought he saw one of the baubles light up on the tree inside the doorway. Putting it down to a trick of the light, he walked to his car as flurries of snow swirled around him.

He had just reached his car when his phone rang. His mum.

'Hi, sweetheart, I'm calling to say, since it's busy here tonight, what with the party, and with the snow coming down heavier, don't you be making that journey up here. Do you hear me? I'm fine. Oh, and I almost forgot, no need to come here tomorrow either. We've been invited to dinner at Sugar and Spice.'

Fraser grinned as gales of laughter sailed down the phone. Yes, his mother definitely had a better social life than him.

'No problem, Mum. And yes, Tabitha told me about tomorrow. Merry Christmas Eve. See you tomorrow. Love you.'

'I love you, too, son.' She hung up.

When he got home, not for the first time he admired the wreath adorning his front door. His mum's thoughtfulness had given him that initial injection of Christmas spirit.

Inside, he put the kettle on and flicked on the Christmas lights. He might not be able to replicate the cosiness of Sugar and Spice, but he'd have a blooming good try. He sent a prayer of thanks to Lara for guilt-tripping him into putting up his tree. It really had made a positive difference to his mood, coming home in the evening and it being there to welcome him.

Turning on his woodburning stove, he enjoyed watching the flickering of the flames as he sat back and thought of the day's events. He had a couple of good bottles of red he could take with him the next day. He'd eat his M&S meal for one on Boxing Day instead. As he sat down to read the book Tabitha had given him, the flames flickered again. He shook his head. He was losing it; he could have sworn he saw letters in the flames. Letters that spelled H O P E.

He set his mug on the coaster and stood up to walk around the room, taking in the falling snow from the six-foot high case-and-sash double-aspect windows. It was like a winter wonderland and he hoped at some point in the future, he could stand here looking out over the river with someone significant to him. Tabitha. He sighed heavily, then his eyes fell upon the mail he'd brought in from behind the door earlier. He'd forgotten it in his haste to set up his cosy Christmas idyll, loath to lose the feeling of contentment that had fallen over him at Sugar and Spice.

He considered not opening the mail until Boxing Day. Who wanted to open bills on Christmas Eve, after all? But his curiosity got the better of him and he opened first his Mastercard bill, then a couple of Christmas cards – Christmas post really was the pits – and finally a brown envelope. When he saw its contents, he sank onto the sofa, his legs almost buckling beneath him.

He'd been promoted. The headteacher job at Ferntree that he'd applied for months ago, well before he was taken on for the post of acting head at Heatherwood, was his. The woman who'd originally been offered the job had had a change in circumstances and was no longer able to take up the post. He could feel the blood drain from his face. Something he thought he'd always wanted, and now, having spent a few months at Heatherwood, it was bittersweet. He was getting on well with the staff, he was friends with Paul, he was proud of the school, and the staff, and he loved the kids. His mind raced with the possibilities. When did they want him to start? Did it even say? Was he to call them? He couldn't take it in. It was such a shock. Was that why the education authority had arranged a meeting at the school in December? Was it to see how he was handling his role at Heatherwood? How he'd coped with a school of his own to run? The questions were endless. He needed to speak to someone about this, but late on Christmas Eve was not the time, nor was there anyone he could talk to, since the education authority was closed until the second week in January.

After his heart rate had returned to normal, he made himself a fresh cup of tea, and although it took him three attempts to get into the book Tabitha had given him, because of everything swirling through his brain, he enjoyed the subject matter and the themes. It was an unusual choice, he felt, but also completely engaging. Tabitha had been right; it was a good choice for any book lover.

He stood up to forage for snacks, and as he did so, a sheet of paper fell from the book. Written on a notelet, in ornate script, were the words, 'Merry Christmas, Fraser. All my love, Tabitha x'

Fraser's heart soared. There was the message he'd wanted, loud and clear. She felt the same way. No more of this feeling like a teenage boy, in uncharted territory, wondering if his feelings were reciprocated. She'd spelled it out for him in black and white. Overcome with emotion, he sat back down heavily on the sofa, and laughed, a wide smile spreading across his face. Something that had seemed out of reach for so long suddenly seemed a very real possibility, and the next day he would be able to spend Christmas with Tabitha and her family, and his own family, too, in the shape of his mum and Stanley, because Stanley, as was plain for all to see, was fast becoming a special friend to his mum. The headmaster job was a sign. Tabitha's note was another sign. And, the icing on the cake was, if he was no longer headmaster at Heatherwood, he would be free to date Tabitha. He'd no longer have a conflict of interest.

Right there, right then, he came to a decision. It was time for him to be proactive about his future and the people in it.

This Christmas, and beyond, was looking a whole lot brighter.

Chapter Twenty-one

'Merry Christmas, Mum.' Lara jumped on the bed. 'Can we go see if Santa has been?'

Her mum rubbed her eyes and sat up, yawning. 'What time is it?'

'Half past six. Santa must have been.'

'OK, let's check.'

Lara thundered downstairs and shouted, 'Santa's been.'

When her mum came in, Lara was almost bouncing with unrestrained energy. 'Can I open my presents?'

'Of course you can, sweetheart.' Her mum sat down on the sofa.

Lara reached for a present. 'This one is from Santa to me,' she said, her voice high with unbridled excitement. 'And this one's for you, from Santa.'

As their piles of opened presents grew, Lara thought about that other thing she'd asked Santa for. She'd need to wait until later, though.

'Merry Christmas, Elaine.' Paul brought her breakfast in bed. 'Bacon rolls, crumpets with lashings of butter and English Breakfast tea.'

'Oh, Merry Christmas, Paul. You do know if you

retired, I could expect this every day, though.'

When Paul raised an eyebrow, she said, 'Kidding! Actually, look at this. I was doing a bit of research on the internet and I found these dresses. Aren't they perfect for a Caribbean cruise?'

Paul sighed inwardly.

'Anyway, did you open your present yet?'

'No. Since when did I open presents without you?'

'Good point. Well, why don't you help me eat this and then we can go find out what I got you?'

Paul didn't let on he'd already had a toasted crumpet and happily helped himself to another. When breakfast was done, he took the tray away and Elaine slipped on her dressing gown and joined him downstairs.

'Right, that big one at the back of the tree, that's yours,' Elaine said. 'It's up to you if you keep it for last or open it now.'

Paul's forehead wrinkled. He was eager to find out what Elaine had bought him that was so big, particularly when she usually bought him aftershave, but equally he liked to tease her a little, and it would wind her up no end to have him wait until the last present to open it.

'Why don't you open some of your presents first?' he said. Like she needed to be asked. She was worse than a kid on Christmas morning. She tore the wrapping off without preamble and Paul settled in for the burst of enthusiasm that was due to follow.

'Oh, I love it.' She withdrew the tiny cayman pendant he'd bought her. 'Because we're going to the Cayman Islands.' She threw her arms around him then said, 'Right, Paul, no more nonsense. Open your present.'

He rolled his eyes then dug around at the back of the

tree and pulled out the large rectangular box.

'I hope you like it,' said Elaine.

As he unveiled its contents, a wide smile broke across his face. 'A Lord of the Rings chess set. Oh, wait until I tell Stanley. He was telling me the other day he liked specialty sets. Thank you.' He kissed his wife on the lips and then started setting up all the pieces.

'Will you play me?' he asked.

'God, no. What would I want to do that for? Ask someone who plays chess.'

He continued admiring and setting up his new chessboard, all the while grinning at the fact that some things would never change.

Valerie sat back as Munro passed her the non-alcoholic Bucks Fizz he'd bought for her.

'Thanks.' She raised her glass to his as they watched Ivy screaming with delight over the gifts she'd received. If the twins weren't already awake, she'd have woken them.

Valerie knew there was nothing better than watching your children open their gifts on Christmas morning. She'd had eight years of Ivy being able to open them on her own, until the twins finally came along earlier this year. The light shining in children's eyes, the pure unadulterated joy of Santa bringing you what you'd asked for took some beating, and looking at Ivy, Santa had come up trumps again. Ivy was already roller-blading around the kitchen and had threatened to make both her and Munro jump rope later, to music.

Valerie looked forward to the chaotic couple of days ahead, and was glad it was only their own little family for

Christmas dinner. With Munro's family in Perthshire and her own parents in Cambridge, they were too spread out for them to have a big get-together on Christmas Day. Munro's parents were heading down on the twenty-eighth to visit and then she, Munro and the children were flying to her parents for two days before Munro had to head to the States.

Christmas Day wasn't the time to tell her husband that she wasn't going back to her job, and that she was going to do what she'd always said she would: open her own interpreting and translation company. She'd got things back on an even keel with Munro from a family perspective; now she had to do the same from a professional standpoint too. She knew he'd support her, but she wanted to have all her ducks in a row first, and it wasn't as if it were a plan that would come to fruition overnight. There was a great deal of planning to do, but she always enjoyed that phase, and she'd love telling her bullying boss where to … but it was Christmas. Suffice to say, he'd be looking for a replacement for her in the New Year.

Next year, she'd take her time, spending quality time with both Ivy and the twins, and then in a couple of years, she'd have everything in place to set up her company. She raised her glass to Munro again. 'Merry Christmas, darling.'

'Merry Christmas, Valerie.' They clinked glasses and sat back, then Munro jumped up as Ivy tried to set up her table tennis table in the living room.

'Merry Christmas, wife,' said Ryan as he stretched across the bed to plant a kiss on Bella's shoulder.

'Merry Christmas, husband.'

'I'm afraid I don't have a big gift for you this year.'

'I don't need a big gift,' said Bella, wrapping her arms around his neck, her long blonde hair falling over his bare chest. 'I need a thoughtful gift.'

'A thoughtful gift?' Ryan pursed his lips and considered her words for a moment. 'OK, how about this?' He leant over and opened the drawer of the bedside table, withdrawing an envelope.

Bella's forehead furrowed and she waited for him to pass it to her. When he offered it and she went to take it, he held it out of her grasp, and then above his head, then he stood up on the bed, and so did Bella, and soon they were wrestling, as Ryan made her work for her present.

'This is harder than going to the gym,' she panted.

'It'll be worth it, I promise.'

'It had better be. A-ha! Got it!'

Ryan lay back with his hands behind his head on the pillow as Bella opened the envelope. When she read what it said, she screamed, 'Oh my God, Ryan. Oh my God, thank you! Thank you!' She crawled the remaining distance on the bed to him and kissed him hard on the mouth.

'You're welcome,' he gasped once she'd finished kissing him. 'Now, will we get up, as I can't wait to surprise your mum and dad for Christmas lunch, plus you need to pack.'

'Pack?' Bella looked at him.

'You didn't read the letter properly, did you, or the tickets?'

Bella reread the letter and the date on the tickets. 'Oh my God. We're going to New York tomorrow?'

'You always said you wanted to ice skate in Central Park in winter. There's also a few other parcels downstairs under the tree. I sneaked them in late last night. You're going to need them.'

'Oh. I love you, Ryan Hopkins.'

'And I love you, Bella Hopkins.' He kissed her long and hard, and when he came up for air, he said, 'And next year, I want us to talk about looking into adoption, if you're sure.'

'I'm sure, Ryan, but you have to be. It's too important,' Bella said.

'Belles.' Ryan took her gently by the arms. 'I can't think of anyone who would make a better mother, and I want you to be the mother of our children. I want us to have children now. Maybe the specialists are wrong. Maybe we can start trying already when we're in the US.'

Bella laughed. 'Is that so if we conceive the baby there, we can call them Madison after Madison Square Garden or after some other venue?'

'Hey, there's a thought. I like the name Madison.' As she shoved him gently, he said, 'No. It's because I don't want to wait any longer. Even if we can't conceive and we end up going down the adoption route, we could still name our baby after a location we've visited. But who knows, maybe this time next year we'll be celebrating our baby's first Christmas.'

Bella's eyes filled with tears and she nuzzled into Ryan's neck. 'If you're sure.'

'I'm sure, Belles. I've never been surer of anything in my life – except when I asked you to marry me.'

Bella drew back from him, looked for confirmation of his sincerity, then jumped up and said, 'Bags me in the shower first then,' and squealed as Ryan launched himself off the bed after her.

When Fraser arrived at Sugar and Spice with Stanley and his mum, everything was already in full swing. Christmas music was playing softly in the background. 'Rockin' Around The Christmas Tree' emanated from somewhere, and Tom and Jerry were sitting at a table that had been set for twenty or so, sipping glasses of champagne, or perhaps it was Prosecco.

As everyone introduced themselves to those they didn't know, Tabitha and Sophie walked through from the kitchen carrying trays of drinks. Fraser stopped in front of Tabitha. Sophie glanced to the side and said, 'I'll take these drinks through. Leave that on the side, Tabitha.'

Tabitha set her tray down on her right and stood in front of Fraser, hands clasped in front of her.

'I got your note,' Fraser said.

'You did?' Tabitha smiled.

'Not at first, but it fell out of the book when I went to make tea.'

'Just as well you went to make tea then.'

'That's what I thought.'

'And?'

'And what?' A smile played on Fraser's lips, but when he saw Tabitha's falter, he said, 'And I thought it was the best news I'd had in ages.' He leant forward and said, 'Merry Christmas, Tabitha,' then kissed her full on the lips, resulting in whoops and wolf whistles from the other side of the café.

'About time too,' said Sophie as she came back with the trays. 'Honestly, you pair, I thought I was going to have to draw you a diagram.'

'Crude, Sophie, but effective,' said Tabitha as she took Fraser's hand in hers and sat down at the table opposite her daughter.

'Hi, Lara,' said Fraser. 'Did you get what you wanted from Santa?'

Lara looked at him then glanced at her mum. 'Yes, thank you. I got *everything* I wanted.'

When she smirked, both her mum and Fraser looked at each other, eyebrows raised, but Lara said nothing further.

'Right, everyone, grub's up,' said Jacob as he, Tabitha and Sophie brought out trays bearing the starters. Silence soon reigned as they all tucked in to the smoked salmon and cream cheese bruschetta, followed by roast goose with all the trimmings, and after a little break, they rounded off the meal with cranberry sauce cake.

When they were all replete, Stanley cleared his throat and said, 'I have something to say.'

Everyone's eyes swivelled to where he was sitting at the far end of the table. Jacob wondered what was coming next.

'Eleven years ago, I lost my wife, Edie, and I never thought I'd enjoy Christmas ever again. Then I met Jacob and Sophie and Tabitha and eventually Lara, too, and that made the world of difference to me, and how I viewed this holiday, and Winstanton, with all its memories.'

He paused as if garnering inner strength from somewhere, then said, 'And this year, I met someone, someone I know Edie would approve of, someone I know Edie would have been best friends with. Now, Una–' he turned to her and took one of her hands in his '–I'm too old to get married, but if I were to get married again, I'd want it to be to you, So, Una–' he then took out a ring box from his pocket and opened it '–I ask this with the same solemnity that I would if I were asking you to be my wife: will you be my best friend and wear this ring as a symbol of our friendship?'

Everyone gawped. All Jacob could think was, *Well done, Stanley.*

Fraser had gone white.

Una, who had initially gaped too, sat back in her chair and said, 'Stanley, I would be honoured to wear your ring.' She patted his hand. 'And I am already your best friend.'

She proffered her hand and Stanley, with some effort, glided the gold Claddagh ring with diamond inserts onto her finger. Then Una leant forward and kissed Stanley on the lips.

Jacob smiled. 'Congratulations. It seems to be a day for announcements.'

When everyone looked at him, he said, 'We have something else to celebrate today, too.' He held up his hands and said, 'Stanley, Una, sorry, I'm not trying to steal your thunder, but Sophie–' he stopped and pulled Sophie towards him '–Sophie's pregnant. We're going to have a baby!'

Everyone cheered and then everyone was standing up and patting Jacob on the back, and congratulating Sophie. Then they did the same with Stanley and Una, and cries of 'you old goat' were heard from Tom or was it Jerry?

Lara took the opportunity when everyone was busy to slip into the kitchen unnoticed. She sighed with relief and happiness. Everything had worked out exactly as it should have.

She took out the antique baby rattle from the little bag

she kept it in, the one her mum thought contained favourite toys. She shook it gently – yes, it was filling back up nicely. She pressed the indentation in its handle and heard, 'Hi, Lara, Merry Christmas.'

'Hi, Natalie. Merry Christmas.'

'Did everything go to plan?'

'Yes, eventually. Thanks for all your help. I was a bit worried for a while there.'

'Lara, sometimes there are challenges and obstacles to overcome, but Christmas spirit always prevails.'

'It really does, especially when helped by not one but two Christmas spirits.'

'Lara, I'll be here again next year to help you if you need me, you know that, but I think you've had a great first year as the Christmas spirit. You deserve a pat on the back.'

'Thanks, Natalie.'

'Oh, did you bring the snow globe?'

'Yes! It's here.' Lara fetched it from where she'd hidden it in one of the kitchen cupboards.

'Right, so if you shake it now, tell me what you see.'

Lara shook the snow globe and watched as the snowflakes settled to reveal Mr and Mrs Hopkins seated at a long dining table, with lots of other people. Two of them looked like Mrs Hopkins. Her mum? Her sister?

'Is that your teacher?' Natalie said in her ear.

'Yes. She looks happy.'

'She is, Lara. Shake the snow globe again. What do you see?'

Lara shook it and Ivy's living room appeared. Ivy was sitting on the floor with her twin brother and sister on either side of her and she was shaking a tiny rattle at each of them. When Lara looked again, Ivy's mum and dad were sitting and lying on the couch, her mum's head against her dad's chest.

'Do they look happy?'

'Yes, really happy.'

'Good job, Lara. Shake again.'

Lara shook the snow globe and this time the scene was outside. Mr Fairbairn and his wife were out walking, all wrapped up, laughing and joking, arm in arm as they walked along the riverside.

'And them?'

'Yes, they look happy too.'

'OK, Lara, one final test. Well, two. You can only shake the snow globe one more time tonight. Are you ready?'

'Yes.' When she shook the snow globe, it showed her everyone in the next room, chatting away, still congratulating her uncle Jacob and aunt Sophie and Una and Stanley, but her eyes were drawn to her mum and Mr McCafferty, who were sitting side by side, whispering and holding hands. Then the view panned back to her, to her watching them, and her face was shining with happiness.

'Lara, are you happy with what you see?'

'Yes, Natalie.'

'Then, kiddo, job done. You'll always have me if you need me, but I think you've got this. Merry Christmas, Lara.'

'Merry Christmas, Natalie.'

But Natalie had gone.

As Lara returned to the room where everyone was enjoying the festivities, she stood tall and nodded to herself.

She did have this. She'd made this happen, with a little help from her friend Natalie. Natalie Hope, the Christmas spirit of the past. Now it was time for Lara to step up not only as the Christmas spirit of the present, but also of the future.

Author's Note

Did you get your free short stories yet?

TWO UNPUBLISHED EXCLUSIVE SHORT STORIES.

Interacting with my readers is one of the most fun parts of being a writer. I'll be sending out a monthly newsletter with new release information, competitions, special offers and basically a bit about what I've been up to, writing and otherwise.

You can get the previously unseen short stories, *Mixed Messages* and *Time Is of the Essence*, FREE if you sign up to my mailing list.
www.susanbuchananauthor.com

Did you enjoy *A Little Christmas Spirit*?

I'd really appreciate if you could leave a review on Amazon. It doesn't need to be much, just a couple of lines. I love reading customer reviews. Seeing what readers think of my books spurs me on to write more. Sometimes I've even written more about characters or created a series because of reader comments. Plus, reviews are SO important to authors. They help raise the profile of the author and make it more likely that the book will be visible on Amazon to more readers. Every author wants their book to be read by more people, and I am no exception!

COMING JANUARY 2025!

The Leap Year Proposal

When three women meet on a mutual friend's hen weekend on the Scottish island of Arran, they get more than they bargained for when one of them has the genius idea of proposing on 29 February, like the age-old Irish tradition.

High-flying businesswoman Anouska and boyfriend Zach are deliriously happy and madly in love. If only they had more time together. But now she's pregnant and doesn't know how to tell him since having kids hadn't featured in their plans.

Dog walker Jess lives with her childhood sweetheart, but they're already like an old married couple, without the romance, or the wedding, or the ring. When Mark doesn't propose on New Year's Eve, Jess is gutted and decides to take matters into her own hands.

Ellie and Scott still live apart after six years, and his lack of commitment is a sore point. She's up for a huge promotion which involves moving country. It's make-or-break time. She needs to know he's worth turning down the job for.

The women meet weekly, helping each other with decisions big and small, becoming each other's support system in the run-up to 'the big ask'.

Will love conquer all or will their hopes and dreams come crashing down around them?

Pre-order via the book page on my website
www.susanbuchananauthor.com

Have you read them all?

The Christmas Spirit

Natalie Hope takes over the reins of the Sugar and Spice bakery and café with the intention of injecting some Christmas spirit. Something her regulars badly need.

Newly dumped Rebecca is stuck in a job with no prospects, has lost her home and is struggling to see a way forward.

Pensioner Stanley is dreading his first Christmas alone without his beloved wife, who passed away earlier this year. How will he ever feel whole again?

Graduate Jacob is still out of work despite making hundreds of applications. Will he be forced to go against his instincts and ask his unsympathetic parents for help?

Spiky workaholic Meredith hates the jollity of family gatherings and would rather stay home with a box set and a posh ready meal. Will she finally realise what's important in life?

Natalie sprinkles a little magic to try to spread some festive cheer and restore Christmas spirit, but will she succeed?

Return of the Christmas Spirit

Christmas is just around the corner when the enigmatic Star begins working at Butterburn library, but not everyone is embracing the spirit of the season.

Arianna is anxious about her mock exams. With her father living abroad and her mother working three jobs to keep them afloat, she doesn't have much support at home.

The bank is threatening to repossess Evan's house, and he has no idea how he will get through Christmas with two children who are used to getting everything they want.

After 23 years of marriage, Patricia's husband announces he's moving out of the family home and moving in with his secretary. Patricia puts a brave face on things, but inside, she's devastated and lost.

Stressed-out Daniel is doing the work of three people in his sales job, plus looking after his kids and his sick wife. Pulled in too many different directions, he hasn't even had a chance to think about Christmas.

Can Star, the library's Good Samaritan, help set them on the path to happiness this Christmas?

Just One Day – Winter

Thirty-eight-year-old Louisa has a loving husband, three wonderful kids, a faithful dog, a supportive family and a gorgeous house near Glasgow. What more could she want?

TIME.

Louisa would like, just once, to get to the end of her never-ending to-do list. With her husband Ronnie working offshore, she is demented trying to cope with everything on her own: the after-school clubs, the homework, the appointments … the constant disasters. And if he dismisses her workload one more time, she may well throttle him.

Juggling running her own wedding stationery business with family life is taking its toll, and the only reason Louisa is still sane is because of her best friends and her sisters.

Fed up with only talking to Ronnie about household bills and incompetent tradesmen, when a handsome stranger pays her some attention on her birthday weekend away, she is flattered, but will she give in to temptation? And will she ever get to the end of her to-do list?

Just One Day – Spring

Mum-of-three Louisa thought she only had her never-ending to-do list to worry about, but the arrival of a ghost from the recent past puts her in an untenable position. Can she navigate the difficult situation she's in without their friendship becoming common knowledge or will it cause long-term damage to her marriage?

When a family member begins to suspect there's more to her relationship with the new sous-chef than meets the eye, Louisa needs to think on her feet or she'll dig herself into a deeper hole. But the cost of keeping her secret, not only from her husband, comes at a high price, one which tugs at her conscience.

With everyday niggles already causing a further rift between Louisa and husband Ronnie, will she manage to keep her family on track whilst her life spirals out of control? And when tragedy strikes, will Ronnie step up when she needs him most?

Just One Day – Summer

List-juggling, business-owner mum-of-three Louisa is reeling after a tragedy, as well as learning how to cope after a life-changing revelation. With oil worker husband Ronnie possibly being able to move onshore, she hopes he can help her manage the burden.

But the secrets she keeps are causing her headaches and she's unsure if her ability to make good decisions has deserted her. All she seems to do is upset those around her.

With Louisa's to-do list gathering pace at an incredible speed, will she manage to provide a stable home for them all, embrace her new normal as well as rebuild their life from what's left?

And if she gets what she has always wanted, will it match up to her expectations?

Just One Day – Autumn

Pregnant Louisa is just getting back on track when life throws her another curveball. Now, it's not a case of how she'll get through her to-do lists but how she'll manage being a mum again.

No one seems to understand. How will she run her company, be partner in a new venture, look after her three kids and handle a newborn? And why does everyone think this will be easy? Except her.

All Louisa wants is to be a good mum, wife, friend, sister and daughter, and have a bit of time left for herself, but sometimes that's too big an ask. Can she find the support she needs, or will she forever be pulled in too many directions, always at the mercy of her to-do lists?

Sign of the Times

Sagittarius – Travel writer Holly heads to Tuscany to research her next book, but when she meets Dario, she knows she's in trouble. Can she resist temptation? And what do her mixed feelings mean for her future with her fiancé?

Gemini – Player Lucy likes to keep things interesting and has no qualms about being unfaithful to her long-term boyfriend. A cardiology conference to Switzerland changes Lucy, perhaps forever. Has she met her match, and is this feeling love?

Holly is the one who links the twelve signs. Are you ready to meet them all?

A tale of love, family, friendship and the lengths we go to in pursuit of our dreams.

The Dating Game

Work, work, work. That's all Glaswegian recruitment consultant Gill does. Her friends fix her up with numerous blind dates, none suitable, until one day Gill decides enough is enough.

Seeing an ad on a bus billboard for Happy Ever After dating agency 'for the busy professional', on impulse, she signs up. Soon she has problems juggling her social life as well as her work diary.

Before long, she's experiencing laughs, lust and ... could it be love? But just when things are looking up for Gill, an unexpected reunion forces her to make an impossible choice.

Will she get her happy ever after, or is she destined to be married to her job forever?